Ben Jonson's A Tale of a Tub: A Retelling

David Bruce

Published by David Bruce, 2022.

BEN JONSON'S A TALE OF A TUB: A RETELLING

First edition. July 10, 2022.

Copyright © 2022 David Bruce.

ISBN: 979-8201050658

Written by David Bruce.

Table of Contents

Dedicated to Carl Eugene Bruce and Josephine Saturday Bruce

***

Educate Yourself

Read Like A Wolf Eats

Be Excellent to Each Other

Books Then, Books Now, Books Forever

***

In this retelling, as in all my retellings, I have tried to make the work of literature accessible to modern readers who may lack some of the knowledge about mythology, religion, and history that the literary work's contemporary audience had.

Do you know a language other than English? If you do, I give you permission to translate this book, copyright your translation, publish or self-publish it, and keep all the royalties for yourself. (Do give me credit, of course, for the original retelling.)

I would like to see my retellings of classic literature used in schools, so I give permission to the country of Finland (and all other countries) to buy (or get free) one copy of this eBook and give copies to all students forever. I also give permission to the state of Texas (and all other states) to buy (or get free) one copy of this eBook and give copies to all students forever. I also give permission to all teachers to buy (or get free) one copy of this eBook and give copies to all students forever.

Teachers need not actually teach my retellings. Teachers are welcome to give students copies of my eBooks as background material. For example, if they are teaching Homer's *Iliad* and *Odyssey*, teachers are welcome to give students copies of my *Virgil's* Aeneid: *A Retelling in Prose* and tell students, "Here's another ancient epic you may want to read in your spare time."

CAST OF CHARACTERS

CHANON HUGH

Vicar of Pancras, and Captain Thumbs.

Chanon Hugh is a petty — of lesser importance — member of the clergy.

"Chanon" is an archaic spelling of "canon." A chanon, or canon, is a clergyman.

Chanon Hugh is sometimes called Sir Hugh; "Sir" was a title given to clergymen as well as to knights.

Pancras is St. Pancras, a parish in Middlesex. It is in the middle of the villages mentioned in Ben Jonson's play, and it is the location of the church.

Pancras is also called Pancridge in Ben Jonson's play.

SQUIRE TRIPOLY TUB

Of Totten Court.

Squire Tub is older than Audrey, who is of an age to be married.

Totten Court is a village.

BASKET HILTS

Squire Tub's serving-man, and his governor.

A basket is a sword guard that is located on the sword's hilt.

A governor is a tutor and protector.

JUSTICE PREAMBLE

Of Maribone, alias Bramble.

Justice Preamble dislikes being called Bramble.

MILES METAPHOR

Justice Preamble's clerk.

LADY TUB

Of Totten Court. Squire Tub's mother.

POL-MARTEN

Lady Tub's gentleman-usher.

A marten is an animal whose fur is valued. An usher escorts and serves a lady.

DIDO WISP

Lady Tub's serving-woman.

In Virgil's Aeneid, *Dido was Queen of Carthage. Read Book 4 of the* Aeneid *for her story.*

TOBIAS "TOBY" TURF

High Constable of Kentish Town.

A High Constable is a senior parish official in charge of constables. They keep the peace.

Kentish Town is a village.

DAME SYBIL TURF

Tobias Turf's wife.

MISTRESS AUDREY TURF

The Turfs' daughter, the bride.

JOHN CLAY

Of Kilburn. Tile-maker, the appointed bridegroom.

Kilburn is a village.

IN-AND-IN MEDLEY

Of Islington. Cooper, joiner, and headborough.

In-and-in is a kind of dice game. A medley is a mixture. A joiner is a carpenter. A cooper makes tubs and barrels. Headboroughs help keep the peace, and they assist constables.

In-and-In Medley is a parody of Inigo Jones, with whom Ben Jonson created masques. The two men argued over who should get the most credit for their collaborations. Two of Inigo Jones' favorite words were "feasible" and "conduce."

Islington is a village.

RASI CLENCH

Of Hampstead. Farrier and petty constable.

Farriers work with horses' hooves, trimming and shoeing them.

A clench is part of a nail used in shoeing horses.

A petty constable is also known as a headborough.

Clench is an older man.

Hampstead is rural; Ben Jonson's play refers to Hampstead Heath.

TO-PAN

Tinker or metal-man of Belsize, thirdborough.

To-Pan works with pans. A thirdborough is a petty constable.

Belsize is a manor in Hampstead.

D'OGENES SCRIBEN

Of Chalcot, the great writer.

Diogenes was an ancient Greek philosopher; he was a Cynic.

Chalcot is a hamlet.

BALL PUPPY

The High Constable's serving-man.

"Ball" is a nickname for "Hannibal"; it is also a common name for a dog. Hannibal was a great Carthaginian general, known for taking African elephants across the Alps to attack Rome.

FATHER ROSIN (and his two boys)

The minstrel, and his two boys.

Rosin is used in lubricating musical bows.

JOAN, JOYCE, MADGE, PARNEL, GRISELL, KATE

Maids of the bridal (wedding feast).

BLACK JACK

The Lady Tub's butler.

"Black Jack" means "beer jug."

TWO GROOMS (serving-men)

THE SCENE: FINSBURY HUNDRED (an open area in Middlesex)

THE TIME: Valentine's Day

THE PLOT: In this play, Mistress Audrey Turf is courted by four men. She is supposed to marry John Clay on this day — Valentine's Day — but other men interfere to prevent that marriage and try to get her to marry someone else. Two of the other men who want to marry her are Squire Tub and Justice Bramble. A fourth man also wants to marry her. (Ball Puppy also inquires whether she could love him, but he is rejected and takes it calmly and marries someone else.)

RUSTIC DIALECT:

Several characters have a rustic dialect, including Ball Puppy, Basket Hilts, John Clay, D'ogenes Scriben, In-and-In Medley, Rasi Clench, and To-Pan.

The major characteristics of the rustic dialect are these:

Z is often but not always used for S

zealed bags o'silver = sealed bags of silver

Zin Valentine = Saint Valentine (in some places, "saint" is pronounced "sin")

deadly zin = deadly sin

V is often used for F

vifty pound = fifty pounds

'un, 'hun, 'hum are the rustic dialect form for *'im, him, them*

'cham means *I am*

'che and *'ch* mean *I* — possibly, *'ch* is related to *ich* (German for "I")

Some R sounds are transposed.

preform = perform

perportions = proportions

NOTES:

In Ben Jonson's society, a tale of a tub meant the same thing as a cock-and-bull story.

A cock-and-bull story is a ridiculous story. The term may have come from two inns that coaches stopped at in Stony Stratford, England. One inn was called the Cock and the other was called the Bull. Travelers would tell outrageous, unbelievable stories to entertain themselves and others.

In Ben Jonson's society, a person of higher rank would use "thou," "thee," "thine," and "thy" when referring to a person of lower rank. (These terms were also used affectionately and between equals.) A person of lower rank would use "you" and "your" when referring to a person of higher rank.

"Sirrah" was a title used to address someone of a social rank inferior to the speaker. Friends, however, could use it to refer to each other.

The word "wench" in Ben Jonson's time was not necessarily negative. It was often used affectionately.

The word "clown" can mean "rustic fellow" as well as "comic fellow."

The phrase "go to" can be imprecatory. These days, it is used in "go to Hell!"

Proverbs are often words of wisdom, but they can also be short pithy sayings in general use. In this sense, they can be clichés.

A hundred is a subdivision of a county or a shire; it has its own court. The setting, of course, is Finsbury Hundred (an open area in Middlesex).

PROLOGUE

No state affairs, nor any politic club

    Pretend [Claim] we in our tale, here, of a tub,

    But acts of clowns [comic rustics] and constables today

    Stuff out the scenes of our ridiculous [funny] play.

    A cooper's wit, or some such busy spark,

    Illumining the High Constable and his clerk

    And all the neighborhood, from old records

    Of antique [old; also possibly "antic," aka funny] proverbs, drawn from Whitsun-lords,

    And their authorities at wakes and ales,

    With country precedents and old wives' tales,

    We bring you now, to show what different things

    The cotes of clowns are from the courts of kings.

***

"Whitsun-lords" are mock-lords who rule at Whitsun, which is the Christian High Holy Day of Pentecost.

    In this context, "wakes" are festivals.

    "Ales" are "ale-drinkings."

    "Cotes of clowns" are the cottages of rustics.

CHAPTER 1
— 1.1 —

Alone, and standing outside Squire Tub's residence in Totten Court, Hugh Chanon, the vicar of Pancras, said to himself on February 14: Valentine's Day:

"Now, by my faith, old BishopValentine, you have brought us nipping weather. Just as the proverb states — 'Februere doth cut and shear' — your day and diocese are very cold.

"All of your parishioners, as well as your lay persons and your quiristers — your choristers — have need to keep to their warm feather-beds if they are provided with loves."

In other words, everyone who already has a husband or wife can stay in bed late and stay warm on Valentine's Day. Those who are without mates need to be stirring.

The choristers are songbirds, which according to folklore, chose their mates on Valentine's Day.

Chanon Hugh continued:

"This is no season to seek new makes in."

"Makes" meant "mates." The word especially applied to birds.

Chanon Hugh continued:

"However, Sir Hugh of Pancras has come hither to Totten Court with news for the young lord of the manor, Squire Tripoly, about his mistress."

Squire Tub was also known as Squire Tripoly. His first name was Tripoly.

In this context, the word "mistress" meant a woman to whom a man was devoted. The word did not necessarily mean a sexual relationship. The Squire wanted to marry this woman.

Vicars were given the honorary title "Sir."

Chanon Hugh called, "What, Squire, I say!"

He continued speaking to himself:

"Tub, I should call him, too.

"Sir Peter Tub was his father, a saltpeter man, who left his mother, Lady Tub of Totten Court, here to revel, and keep open house in; with the young Squire her son, and his governor Basket Hilts, both by sword and dagger."

Some swords and daggers had basket hilts that protected the hand.

Saltpeter is potassium nitrate, which is used in making gunpowder.

He called, "*Domine Armiger* Tub! Squire Tripoly! *Expergiscere*!"

This meant, "Lord Squire Tub! Squire Tripoly! Wake up!"

An *armiger* is a person who is entitled to heraldic arms; that is, the person is someone who is entitled to have a coat of arms.

Chanon Hugh continued:

"I dare not call aloud lest Lady Tub should hear me and think I conjured up the spirit, her son, in priest's lack-Latin. Oh, she is jealous of all mankind for him."

In this context, "jealous" meant "suspicious," and so she was carefully guarding her son. Lady Tub was vigilant in looking out for the well-being of her son.

A "lack-Latin" is a person who doesn't know Latin well. Some priests of the time were ill-educated.

Squire Tub appeared at a window and said, "Chanon, is it you?"

"Yes, it is the Vicar of Pancras, Squire Tub! Wa'hoh!"

"Wa'hoh" is a cry made by a falconer.

Squire Tub said, "I come, I stoop to the call, Sir Hugh! I come in answer to your falconer's call."

"Stoop" meant "swoop down."

He disappeared from the window above and came down in his night clothes.

Chanon Hugh said, "He knows my lure is from his love, fair Audrey, the High Constable's daughter of Kentish Town here. The High Constable is Master Tobias Turf."

Audrey Turf was a maiden of an age to be married, and many men in the area were well aware of that, Squire Tub among them.

"What news comes from Tobias Turf?" Squire Tub asked.

Chanon Hugh answered:

"He has awakened me an hour before I would usually get up, sir. And my duty is to the young worship of Totten Court, Squire Tripoly, who has my heart, as I have his.

"Your mistress — Audrey Turf — is to be made away from you, this morning, St. Valentine's Day.

"A knot of clowns, aka rustics, the Council of Finsbury, so they are y-styled — styled, aka titled — met at her father's.

"All the wise of the hundred there met together: Old Rasi Clench of Hampstead, petty constable; In-and-In Medley, cooper and headborough of Islington; with loud To-Pan, the tinker, or metal-man of Belsize, and a thirdborough; and D'ogenes Scriben, the great writer of Chalcot."

A hundred is a division of a county. All the great men of the hundred had met together to make a decision about an important matter.

"And why did all these wise men meet?" Squire Tub asked.

Chanon Hugh answered, "Sir, to decide in council who shall be a husband or a make — a mate — for Mistress Audrey. That person they have named and chosen: He is John Clay of Kilburn, a tough young fellow, and a tile-maker."

"And what must he do?" Squire Tub asked.

Chanon Hugh answered:

"Cover her, they say, and keep her warm, sir."

One meaning of "cover" is "have sex with."

Chanon Hugh continued:

"Mistress Audrey Turf last night did draw John Clay's name to be her Valentine."

In this society, Valentines were traditionally awarded by chance: the picking of lots.

Chanon Hugh continued:

"This chance occurrence has so taken her father and mother — because they themselves drew lots that matched them so, on Valentine's Eve thirty years ago — that they will have her married today by any means.

"They have sent a messenger to Kilburn, post-haste, for John Clay; which when I knew, I came post-haste with the like message to worshipful Tripoly, the Squire of Totten Court: and my advice is to cross and counteract it."

Chanon Hugh wanted Squire Tub, not John Clay, to be the man who married Audrey.

"What is it, Sir Hugh?" Squire Tub asked.

"Where is your governor Hilts?" Chanon Hugh asked. "Basket must do it."

Basket Hilts would help in the plot to get Squire Tub married to Audrey. Basket Hilts was Squire Tub's governor: his tutor and protector.

"Basket shall be called," Squire Tub said.

He called, "Hilts! Can you see to rise?"

Basket Hilts called from inside Squire Tub's house, "'Cham [I am] not blind, sir, with too much light."

"Open your other eye, and see if it is day," Squire Tub said.

Basket Hilts answered, "'Che [I] can spy that at as little a hole as another, through a millstone."

Two proverbs of the time were these: 1) "One may see daylight at a little hole," and 2) "I can see as far into a millstone as another man."

Squire Tub said to Hugh Chanon, "He will have the last word, even though he talk bilk for it."

"Bilk?" Chanon Hugh said. "What's that mean?"

"Why, nothing," Squire Tub said. "It is a word signifying nothing, and it is borrowed here to express nothing."

"A fine device!" Chanon Hugh said.

"Yes, until we hear a finer," Squire Tub said. "What's your device now, Chanon Hugh?"

A device can be a trick, a plan, and/or a plot. And a bilk can be a hoax or a person who is a cheat.

Chanon Hugh said, "I will tell you in private. Lend it your ear. I will not trust the air with it, or scarcely my shirt; my cassock shall not know it. If I thought it did, I'd strip it off and burn it."

A cassock is a full-length clerical garment.

Squire Tub replied, "That's the way. You have thought up a plan to get a new one, Hugh. Is it worth it? Let's hear it first."

"Then hearken and receive it," Chanon Hugh said.

They whispered together as Chanon Hugh told Squire Tub his plan for getting Audrey and Squire Tub married to each other.

Chanon Hugh said, "That is the plan, sir. Do you relish it?"

Basket Hilts entered the scene, and walked nearby, making himself ready — he was finishing getting dressed — to be of service.

"If Hilts is secret enough to carry it, there's all," Squire Tub said.

Basket Hilts said:

"It is no sand, nor buttermilk?"

These items are difficult to carry without containers.

He continued:

"If't be, Ich'am [I am] no zieve [sieve], or wat'ring-pot, to draw knots i'your 'casions. If you trust me, zo. If not, praform [perform] it your zelves. 'Cham no man's wife, but resolute Hilts. You'll vind me i'the butt'ry."

Knots are criss-crossing lines made by water pouring from watering pots.

"Draw knots in your occasions" means "make difficulties in your business."

"'Cham no man's wife" means "I am no man's wife," aka "I depend on no one." In this context, "wife" means "dependant."

A buttery is a place where alcoholic drinks such as ale are stored.

Basket Hilts exited.

Squire Tub said:

"He is a testy clown, but a clown as tender — soft — as wool, and as melting as the weather in a thaw!

"He'll weep like all April, but he'll roar and bluster at you like middle March before. He will be as mellow, and as tipsy, too, as October; and as grave and bound up like a frost, with the new year, in January.

"He is as rigid as he is rustic."

A proverb stated, "A windy March and a rainy April make a beautiful May."

October was the traditional month for brewing ale.

Chanon Hugh said, "You know his nature, and describe it well. I'll leave him to your managing."

Squire Tub said, "Wait, Sir Hugh; take a good angel with you for your guide, and let this guard you homeward, as the blessing to our plan."

Squire Tub, who was punning on "guardian angel," gave Chanon Hugh a gold coin that was known as an angel. Such coins were stamped with the image of an angel.

Chanon Hugh said:

"I thank you, Squire's worship, most humbly —"

Squire Tub exited.

Chanon Hugh continued:

"— for the next angel: for this angel I am sure of.

"Oh, for a choir of these voices now, to chime in a man's pocket, and cry chink! One does not chirp: It makes no harmony."

Chanon Hugh hoped for more angels to chink in his moneybag and make beautiful music.

He continued:

"Grave Justice Bramble next must contribute an angel. His charity must offer at this wedding.

"I'll bid more to the basin and the bride-ale, although only one can bear away the bride."

At the bride-ale — wedding-feast — gifts were cast into a basin or bowl.

He was offering to give a gift at a second wedding; if a second wedding should be proposed, he hoped to get money from a second suitor.

Chanon Hugh continued:

"I smile to think how like a lottery these weddings are.

"Clay has Audrey in his possession.

"Squire Tub hopes to circumvent the tile-maker John Clay and marry Audrey.

"And now, if Justice Bramble do come off — pay up — it is two to one but Tub may lose his bottom and not marry Audrey."

Justice Preamble, whom many people called Justice Bramble, was a third man who hoped to marry Audrey.

A "bottom" is a "deep place." Women have a deep place.

Chanon Hugh was not loyal to Squire Tub. If he could get money by serving Justice Bramble, he would.

Chanon Hugh exited.

Rasi Clench, In-and-In Medley, D'ogenes Scriben, To-Pan, and Ball Puppy were standing outside Tobias Turf's house in Kentish Town.

Clench of Hampstead was a farrier and petty constable.

Medley was the cooper of Islington and a headborough.

To-Pan of Belsize was a tinker, aka metal-man.

Scriben of Chalcot was a writer.

The Council of Finsbury — the "wise" ones of Finsbury — consisted of In-and-In Medley, Rasi Clench, To-Pan, and D'ogenes Scriben.

Ball Puppy was the High Constable's serving-man.

Remembering what day it was, and what happened thirty years ago on that day, Clench said, "Why, it is thirty years, even as this day now, Zin [Saint] Valentine's Day, of all kursined [christened, aka Christian] days, see. And the zame day of the month, as this Zin Valentine, or I am voully deceived —"

Medley interrupted, "— that our High Constable, Master Tobias Turf, and his dame were married. I think you are right. But what was that Zin Valentine? Did you ever know 'un [him], goodman Clench?"

Clench answered, "Zin Valentine, he was a deadly Zin, and dwelt at Highgate, as I have heard, but it was avore [before] my time. He was a cooper, too, as you are, Medley, an In-an'-In: a woundy brag — an extremely spirited — young vellow, as the 'port [report] went o'hun [of him] then, and in those days."

Scriben asked, "Didn't he write his name as 'Sim Valentine'? Vor I have met no 'Sin' in Finsbury books, and yet I have writ 'em six or seven times over."

Scriben may be the clerk who keeps the Finsbury records. And/or he may have meant to say that he has read the records six or seven times.

To-Pan said, "Oh, you mun [must] look for the nine deadly Sims in the church books, D'oge: not the High Constable's, nor in the county's. Zure [To be sure], that same Zin Valentine, he was a stately and noble Zin, if he were a Zin, and kept brave house —"

"Kept brave house" means "provided splendid hospitality."

The seven deadly sins are anger, envy, gluttony, greed, lust, pride, and sloth.

To-Pan was confusing church theological books with the church books that recorded such things as births, marriages, and deaths.

Clench interrupted:

"— at the Cock and Hen Inn in Highgate.

"You have 'freshed my rememory [refreshed my memory] well in it, neighbor Pan. He had a place in the last King Harry's time, of sorting and matching all the young couples: joining them, and putting them together; which is yet praformed, as on his day — Zin Valentine, as being the Zin of the shire, or the whole county. I am old rivet still, and bear a brain, the clench, the varrier [farrier], and true leech [physician] of Hampstead."

An old rivet is an old fastening — a kind of nail. Old nails are still usable, and Clench's brain was still usable.

A clench is a part of a nail that is turned back when one wants to clench: to fasten more securely.

The last King Harry was King Henry VIII, but Saint Valentine lived long before Henry VIII's time.

To-Pan said, "You are a shrewd and keen-witted antiquity [antiquary], neighbor Clench, and a great guide to all the parishes! The very bell-wether of the hundred, here, as I may zay."

A bell-wether is a leading sheep; it wears a bell and makes noise.

To-Pan continued, "Master Tobias Turf, the High Constable, would not miss you, for a score on [of] us, when he do 'scourse [discourse] of the great Charty [Magna Carta] to us."

This was a compliment: Tobias Turf would not take twenty fellows for one Clench.

In 1215, King John I of England agreed to the bill of rights in the Magna Carta. It recognized some rights for barons, some of whom were rebelling, and for the Church.

Puppy asked, "What's that, a horse? Can 'scourse naught but a horse?"

"'scourse" can mean horse trading in addition to discourse.

Puppy continued, "I never read o'hun [about him], and that in Smithveld Horse Fair — Charty? —"

Puppy was interpreting "Charty" [Carta] as meaning "carthorse."

Puppy continued, "— in the old Fabian's *Chronicles*; nor I think in any more chronicles of more recent times. He may be a giant there, for aught [anything] I know."

Robert Fabian wrote history books about the time up to Henry VII.

"You should do well to study records, fellow Ball, both law and poetry," Scriben said.

Puppy replied, "Why, all's but writing and reading, is it, Scriben? If it is any more, it's mere cheating zure [to be sure], vlat [flat] cheating; all your law and poets, too."

According to some philosophic critics such as Plato, poets and artists create works of art that are far removed from reality: They are mere imitations of reality.

"Master High Constable comes," To-Pan said.

Puppy said, "I'll zay't avore 'hun. [I'll say it before him.]"

Tobias Turf, the High Constable of Kentish Town and the father of Audrey, entered the scene and said, "What's that which makes you all so merry and loud, sirs, huh? I could have heard you all the way to my privy walk [private garden]."

Clench said, "A contervarsy 'twixt [controversy between] your two learned men here: 'Annibal [Hannibal] Puppy says that law and poetry are both flat [completely] cheating. All's but writing and reading, he says, be it verse or prose."

Tobias Turf said, "I think in conzience, he do' zay true! Who is it do thwart'un [contradict him], huh?"

"Why, my friend Scriben, if it please Your Worship," Medley said.

Tobias Turf said:

"Who, D'oge? My D'ogenes? A great writer, by the Virgin Mary! He'll vace me down and put me down, me myself sometimes, and say that verse goes upon veet [feet], as you and I do.

"But I can gi' 'un [give him] the hearing; zit me down and laugh at 'un; and to myself conclude that the greatest clerks [scholars] are not the wisest men ever.

"Here they are both! What, sirs, disputin', and holdin' arguments of [about] verse and prose?

"And no green thing afore [before] the door that shows or speaks [announces] a wedding?"

Greenery was used as decorations during times of celebration such as weddings.

Scriben said, "Those were verses now that your Worship spoke, and they run upon vive [five] feet."

Indeed, some of Tobias Turf's dialogue could be divided into lines that were pentameters and so had five metrical feet.

Tobias Turf said, "Feet, vrom [from] my mouth, D'oge? Leave your 'zurd upinions [absurd opinions] and get me in some boughs to serve as decorations."

Scriben said, "Let 'em have leaves first. There's nothing green but bays and rosemary."

It was February, after all, and so boughs did not have green leaves. Bay leaves and rosemary do not grow on boughs.

"And they're too good for strewings, your maids say," Puppy said.

Tobias Turf said:

"You take up 'dority [authority] still to vouch [cite] against me. All the twelve smocks [women] in the house, to be zure, are your authors.

"Get some fresh hay then, to lay under foot. Get some holly and ivy to make vine [fine (and entwine)] the posts.

"Isn't it Son Valentine's day, and isn't Mistress Audrey, your young dame, to be married?"

Puppy exited to get the required plants.

Tobias Turf then said:

"I marvel that Clay should be so tedious [late in coming]; he's to play Son Valentine, and the clown [rustic] sluggard's not come fro' [from] Kilburn yet!"

Medley asked, "Do you call your son-i'-law a clown, if it please Your Worship?"

Tobias Turf answered:

"Yes, and vor [for] worship — out of respect — too, my neighbor Medley.

"He is a Middlesex clown, and one of Finsbury: They were the first colons of the kingdom here, the primitory [primary] colons, my D'ogenes says.

"Where's D'ogenes, my writer, now? Who were those you told me, D'ogenes, who were the first colons [he meant 'colonists'] of the country? The ones whom the Romans brought in here?"

Scriben said, "The English word 'clown' comes from the Latin word *coloni*. Sir, *colonus* is an inhabitant, a clown original: as you'd zay, a farmer, a tiller of the earth, e'er sin' [ever since] the Romans planted their colony first, which was in Middlesex."

Tobias Turf said:

"Why so!

"I thank you heartily, good D'ogenes, you have zertified me and confirmed what I said. I had rather be an ancient colon, as they zay, a clown of Middlesex, a good rich farmer, or High Constable.

"I'd play [wager] hun 'gain [him against] a knight, or a good squire, or gentleman of any other county in the kindom [kingdom (and population)]."

To-Pan said:

"Outcept [Except] Kent, for there they landed all gentlemen, and came in with the Conqueror, mad Julius Caesar, who built Dover castle.

"My ancestor To-Pan beat the first kettle-drum avore 'hun [him], here vrom Dover on the march."

In this society some people incorrectly thought that Julius Caesar had built the Tower of London. It was actually founded as part of the 1066 Norman Conquest. After Caesar's time, the Romans built a fort at Dover.

To-Pan was mixing up William the Conqueror and Julius Caesar, and he was mixing up the fort at Dover and the Tower of London.

To-Pan continued:

"Which piece of monumental copper [the kettle-drum] hangs up, scoured, at Hammersmith yet; for there they came over the Thames at a low-water mark, vore [before] either London, aye, or Kingston Bridge, I doubt, were kursined [blessed]."

Ball Puppy returned with John Clay, who was supposed to marry Audrey on this Valentine's Day.

Tobias Turf said:

"Zee, who is here: John Clay! Zon Valentine, and bridegroom!

"Have you zeen your Valentine-bride yet, sin' you came, John Clay?"

John Clay was from Kilburn; he was a tile-maker, and he had been appointed to be the bridegroom to Audrey Turf.

"No, wusse [certainly]," John Clay said. "Che [I] alighted, I, just now in the yard. Puppy has scarce unswaddled my legs yet."

Tobias Turf said:

"What, wisps o'your wedding-day, zon?"

John Clay had twisted hay around his stockings to protect his inner legs from chaffing. He was wearing shoes instead of high riding boots that would have protected his legs.

Ball Puppy had helped him remove the hay.

Tobias Turf continued:

"This is right originous [original and natural] Clay, and Clay of Kilburn, too! I would have had boots on this day, zure, zon John."

John Clay explained, "I did it to save charges [costs]. We mun [must] dance, on this day, zure, and who can dance in boots? No, I got on my best straw-colored stockings, and swaddled them over to zave charges, I."

Tobias Turf said:

"And his new chamois doublet, too, with points!"

Points are laces that connect stockings to a doublet (a jacket).

Sausage-hose, which will be mentioned next, are stuffed stockings that resemble sausages.

Tobias Turf continued:

"I like that yet; and his long sausage-hose, like the commander of four smoking tile-kils [tile-kilns], which he is captain of, captain of Kilburn; Clay with his hat turned up, of the leer [larboard, aka port, aka left] side, too, as if he would leap [have sex with] my daughter yet before night, and spring a new Turf to the old house!"

The bridal maidens, carrying rosemary and bay, entered the scene.

Seeing them, Tobias Turf said, "Look, an [if] the wenches ha' not vound 'un [found him] out and do parzent 'un [present him] with a van [fan] of rosemary and bays, to vill [fill] a bow-pot [bouquet], trim the head of my best vore-horse [fore- or front-horse that leads the team]! We shall all have bride-laces or points, I zee; my daughter will be valiant, and prove a very Mary Ambry in the business."

Bride-laces are laces or ribbons that are used to tie some rosemary to be worn at a wedding. Points are laces. Both points and bride-laces were given to wedding guests.

Mary Ambry was a valiant woman who was celebrated in a ballad about the capture of Ghent.

Clench said, "They zaid Your Worship had 'sured her [had promised her] to Squire Tub of Totten Court here; all the hundred rings of it."

According to gossip in Finsbury Hundred, Audrey Turf had been engaged to marry Squire Tub.

Tobias Turf said:

"That's a tale of a tub, sir, a mere tale of a tub. Lend it no ear, I pray you [please]. The Squire Tub is a fine man, but he is too fine a man, and has a Lady Tub, too, to [for] his mother. I'll deal with none of these vine [fine] silken Tubs.

"I prefer John Clay and cloth-breech [homespun clothing] for my money and daughter."

Squire Tub was from a family of a higher social class than the Turf family, and so Tobias Turf did not want his daughter to marry him.

Father Rosin, a musician, and two boys entered the scene.

Seeing him, Tobias Turf said:

"Here comes another old boy, too, vor his colors, will stroke down my wive's udder of purses empty of all her milk-money this winter quarter."

Father Rosin will stroke musical instruments with a bow, and he will be paid for his music with the money Tobias Turf's wife had gotten from selling milk. This will empty her purse of money.

Of course, there is a bawdy meaning in "stroke down my wive's udder."

Tobias Turf continued:

"He is old Father Rosin, the chief minstrel here, chief minstrel, too, of Highgate. She has hired him and all his two boys for a day and a half, and now they come for ribanding and rosemary. Give them enough, girls, give them enough, and take it out in his tunes anon [quickly]."

The girls will give old Father Rosin and his two boys ribanding and rosemary, and old Father Rosin will repay them with music. A riband is a ribbon.

Clench said, "I'll ha' [have] the song 'Tom Tiler,' for our John Clay's sake, and the tile-kils, zure."

Medley the joiner said, "And I'll ha' the song 'The Jolly Joiner,' for my own sake."

To-Pan the tinker said, "I'll ha' 'The Jovial Tinker' for To-Pan's sake."

"We'll all be jovy [jovial] this day vor Son Valentine, my sweet son John's sake," Tobias Turf said.

"There's another reading now," Scriben said. "My master reads it Son and not Sin Valentine."

John Clay is Audrey's Valentine, Tobias Turf wants John Clay to be his son-in-law, and so John Clay is Son Valentine.

"Nor Zim," Puppy said. "And he is in the right; he is High Constable. And who should read above 'un ['im], or avore 'hun [before him]?"

Tobias Turf said:

"Son John shall bid us all welcome on this day. We'll zerve under his colors. Lead the troop, John.

"And Puppy, see the bells ring. Press [Impress, aka enlist] all noises [bands of musicians] of Finsbury, in our name.

"D'ogenes Scriben shall draw a score of warrants vor the business.

"Does any wight parzent [person represent] Her Majesty's person this hundred, 'bove the High Constable?"

"No, no," the others said.

"Use our authority then to the utmost on't [in this business]," Tobias Turf said.

They exited.

Chanon Hugh (the vicar of Pancras) and Justice Preamble talked together.

"So you are sure, sir, to prevent [forestall] 'em all," Chanon Hugh said, "and throw a block [an obstacle] in the bridegroom's way, John Clay, that he will hardly leap over."

Justice Preamble replied, "I conceive [understand] you, Sir Hugh; as if your rhetoric would say, whereas the father of her is a Turf, a very superficies [surface layer] of the earth, he aims no higher than to match in Clay and there has pitched his rest."

"Has pitched his rest" means "has staked everything."

"Right, Justice Bramble," Chanon Hugh said. "You have the winding [devious] wit, encompassing all."

Justice Preamble said:

"Subtle [Cunning] Sir Hugh, you now are in the wrong, and err with the whole neighborhood, I must tell you, for you mistake my name.

"'Justice Preamble' is how I write myself; which with the ignorant clowns here — because of my profession of the law, and place of the peace [my job as judge] — is taken to be Bramble.

"But all my warrants, sir, do run Preamble: Richard Preamble."

"Sir, I thank you for it," Chanon Hugh said. "I thank you that Your good Worship would not let me run longer in error but would take me up thus."

Justice Preamble said, "You are my learned and canonic neighbor; I would not have you stray. But the incorrigible nott-headed beast, the clowns or constables, still let them graze, eat salads, chew the cud. All the town music will not move a log."

"Nott-headed" means "with close-cropped hair," but "nott-headed," of course, sounds like "knot-headed."

Logs have knots.

Amphion was able to build the walls of the ancient Greek city Thebes by playing his lyre. As a result of the music, huge stones moved themselves into the correct position.

Chanon Hugh said, "The beetle and wedges will, where you will have them."

A proverb stated, "There goes the wedge where the beetle drives."

A beetle is a kind of hammer that is used with a wedge to split wood.

"True, true, Sir Hugh," Justice Preamble said.

Miles Metaphor entered the scene.

Seeing Metaphor, Justice Preamble said, "Here comes Miles Metaphor, my clerk. He is the man who shall carry it, Chanon, by my instructions."

Metaphor would help them carry out a plan to get Justice Preamble married to Audrey Turf.

Chanon Hugh said, "He will do it *ad unguem*, Miles Metaphor! He is a pretty fellow."

"*Ad unguem*" means "to perfection." The Latin translation is "to the fingernail." Sculptors would scrape a fingernail over stone to check for flaws.

Justice Preamble said:

"I don't love to keep shadows, or halfwits, to foil [frustrate] a business.

"Metaphor, have you see a king ride forth in state?"

"Sir, that I have," Metaphor said. "King Edward, our late liege and sovereign lord, and I have set down the pomp."

King Edward VI died in 1553. Metaphor had taken notes on the pomp that was on display when King Edward VI had ridden forth in state.

Justice Preamble said:

"Therefore I asked you.

"Have you observed the Messengers of the Chamber, what habits — liveries — they were in?"

The Messengers of the Chamber carried messages, of course, but they also had the legal power to make arrests.

Metaphor answered, "Yes, minor surcoats emblazoned with coats of arms. To the guard, a dragon and a greyhound, for the supporters of the arms."

In other words, the dragon and greyhound were on either side and holding up the shield bearing the coat of arms. "To the guard" means "full-face."

"Well noticed!" Justice Preamble said. "Do you know any of the Messengers of the Chamber?"

Metaphor said, "I know one who dwells here in Maribone."

Justice Preamble asked, "Have you enough acquaintance with him that you could borrow his coat for an hour?"

"Or just his badge," Metaphor said. "It will serve; it's a little thing he wears on his breast."

Justice Preamble said to Metaphor, "His coat, I say, is of more authority. Borrow his coat for an hour."

He said to Chanon Hugh, "I love to do all things completely and perfectly, Chanon Hugh."

He said to Metaphor, "Borrow his coat, Miles Metaphor, or borrow nothing."

Metaphor said, "The tabard — official coat — of his office I will call it, or the coat-armor of his place, and so insinuate with him by that trope."

"Coat-armor" is a heraldic garment worn over armor.

"Insinuate" means "suggest indirectly."

A "trope" is a figure of speech.

Metaphor was going to borrow the coat by using rhetorical flourishes.

This particular coat was worn by a person who had the power to make arrests: a pursuivant. Therefore, we can assume that Justice Preamble and Chanon Hugh's plot involved making an arrest or threatening to make an arrest.

Justice Preamble said, "I know your powers of rhetoric, Metaphor. Fetch him off in a fine figure of speech for his coat, I say."

Metaphor exited to carry out his errand.

Chanon Hugh said, "I'll take my leave, sir, of Your Worship, too, because I may expect the issue of our plan soon."

Justice Preamble said, "Wait, my diviner counsel. Take your fee."

He gave Chanon Hugh some money and said:

"We who take fees allow them to our counsel, and to our prime learned counsel, we allow double fees.

"There are a brace of angels — a pair of gold coins — to support you in your foot-walk this frost, for fear of falling, or spraining of a point of matrimony, when you come at it."

The "spraining of a point of matrimony" means "misinterpreting the marriage laws."

The marriage laws would be misinterpreted (if needed) in such a way as to allow Chanon Hugh to marry Justice Preamble and Audrey Turf to each other.

No one had actually proposed to Audrey Turf. Her bridegroom, John Clay, had been chosen for her.

"I am in Your Worship's service," Chanon Hugh said. "That the exploit is done, and you possessed of Mistress Audrey Turf —"

Justice Preamble interrupted, "I like your plan."

He exited.

Alone, Chanon Hugh said:

"And I like this effect of two to one."

Squire Tub had tipped him only one angel, but Justice Preamble had tipped him two angels.

Chanon Hugh continued:

"It works in my pocket against the Squire, and his half bottom [half-assed undertaking] here, of half a piece [a piece was a coin worth either 20 or 22 shillings, depending on when it was minted], which was not worth the stepping over the stile for."

Justice Preamble tipped better than Squire Tub, and so Chanon Hugh would serve Justice Preamble.

Chanon Hugh continued:

"Squire Tub's mother has quite marred him. Lady Tub is such a vessel of *faeces*; she is all dried earth! *Terra damnata*! She has not a drop of salt or peter in her!"

Terra damnata is a name for the sediment that is left over after an alchemical process. Both *faeces* and *terra damnata* are sediment.

Lady Tub was over-protective of her son.

Chanon Hugh continued:

"All her niter is gone."

"Niter" is "saltpeter." It is also nitrate fertilizer.

Lady Tub had no drop of peter and no fertilizer in her.

A drop of peter (semen) can be fertile.

Her late husband's name was Peter Tub.

Chanon Hugh exited.

Lady Tub of Totten Court (Squire Tub's mother), and Pol-Marten (her usher, aka male attendant) talked together.

Lady Tub said:

"Is the horse ready, Marten? Call my son the Squire.

"This frosty morning we will take the air about the fields; for I do mean to be somebody's Valentine, in my velvet gown, this morning, even though it should be but a beggar-man.

"Why do you stand still, and do not call my son?"

Pol-Marten answered:

"Madam, if he had lain down with the lamb, he would have no doubt been stirring with the lark. But he sat up at play and watched the cock until his first warning scolded him off to rest.

"Late watchers are no early wakers, madam.

"But if Your Ladyship will have him called —"

Lady Tub said:

"Will I have him called? Why did I, sir, order that he be called, you weasel, you vermin of an usher?

"You will return your wit to your first style — title — of Martin Polecat, as a result of these stinking tricks, if you do use them."

Polecats were known for their offensive stink.

Lady Tub continued:

"I shall no more call you Pol-Marten, by the title of a gentleman, if you go on like this —"

"I am gone," Pol-Marten said.

He exited.

Shouting after him, Lady Tub said:

"Be quick then, in your come off — your return — and make amends, you stoat!"

She then said to herself:

"Was there ever such a foumart as serve as an usher to a great worshipful lady, such as myself!"

A foumart is a foul marten. A marten is a weasel-like animal, as is a polecat.

She continued:

"Who, when I heard his name first, Martin Polecat — a stinking name, and not to be pronounced without an apologetic bow in any lady's presence — my very heart even grieved, seeing the fellow young, pretty, and handsome, being then, I say, a basket-carrier, and a man condemned to the saltpeter works.

"I made it my suit to Master Peter Tub that I might change the man's name and position, and call him as I do now, by Pol-Marten, to have it sound like a gentleman in an official position, and I made him my own foreman, my daily waiter."

A "foreman" is a servant who walks ahead of his employer. Waiters are servants.

She continued:

"And he to serve me thus! Ingratitude beyond the coarseness yet of any clownage shown to a lady!"

Pol-Marten returned.

Lady Tub asked him, "What now, is he stirring?"

"He is stirring early out of his bed and ready," Pol-Marten said.

"And so then he is coming?" Lady Tub asked.

"No, madam, he is gone," Pol-Marten said.

"Gone!" Lady Tub said. "To where? Ask the porter where he has gone."

"I met the porter and have asked him about him," Pol-Marten said. "The porter says he let Squire Tub go forth an hour ago."

"An hour ago!" Lady Tub said. "What business could he have so early? Where is his serving-man, grave Basket Hilts, his guide and governor?"

"Gone with his master," Pol-Marten said.

Lady Tub said:

"Has he gone, too?

"Oh, that same surly knave is his indispensable right-hand man, and he leads my son amiss. He has carried him to some drinking match or other.

"Pol-Marten — I will call you so again, I'm friends with you now — go, get your horse and ride to all the towns about here where his haunts are, and cross the fields to meet and bring me word of where he is. He cannot be gone far, being on foot.

"Be curious — careful and diligent — to inquire about him, and tell Wisp, my serving-woman, to come and wait on me."

Pol-Marten exited to carry out his orders.

Lady Tub said to herself, "We mothers bear our sons we have bought with pain, and this makes us often view them with too worriful eyes, and look over them with a zealous fear, beyond what is fitting."

She was aware of her shortcoming, but she was unable to resist it.

Dido Wisp, Lady Tub's serving-woman, arrived on the scene.

"How are you now, Wisp!" Lady Tub said. "Have you a Valentine yet? I'm taking the air to choose one."

"May Fate send Your Ladyship a fit one then," Wisp replied.

"What kind of one is that?" Lady Tub said.

Wisp answered, "A proper — handsome — man to please Your Ladyship."

Lady Tub said:

"Away with that vanity that takes the foolish eye!

"I rather wish for any poor creature whose want may need my alms or courtesy; so Bishop Valentine left us his example to do deeds of charity:

"To feed the hungry, clothe the naked, visit the weak and sick, entertain the poor, and give the dead a Christian funeral.

"These were the works of piety Bishop Valentine practiced, and bade us imitate them, and not look for lovers, or handsome images to please our senses.

"Please, Wisp, deal freely with me now. We are alone, and we may be merry a little.

"Thou are not one of the court glories, aka great women at court, nor are thou one of the wonders for wit and intelligence or for beauty in the city.

"Tell me, what man would satisfy thy present fancy, had thy ambition the ability to choose a Valentine within the queen's dominion, with the provision that he be a subject of the queen's?"

Wisp answered:

"You have given me a large scope, madam, I confess, and I will deal with Your Ladyship sincerely. I'll utter my whole heart to you.

"I would have him be the bravest, the richest, and the properest — the most handsome — man a tailor could make up; or all the poets, along with the makers of perfumes."

The bravest man could be the most splendidly dressed (as a tailor could make him) or the most courageous (as an epic poet or writer of romances could make him).

Wisp continued:

"I would have him be such as not another woman but should feel spite and anger toward me!

"Three city ladies should run mad for him, and an infinite number of country madams."

Lady Tub said, "You'd spare me and let me hold my wits and not run after him?"

Wisp said:

"I should with you — for the young squire, my master's sake — dispense and concede a little; but it should be very little.

"Then all the court-wives I'd have be jealous of me, and all their husbands I'd have be jealous of them. And every lawyer's puss — wench — of any quality would lick her lips for a snatch in the term-time when the law courts are busy."

In this context, "snatch" means a quick treat of a sexual nature — in other words, a quickie.

Lady Tub said:

"Come, let's walk; we'll hear the rest as we go on.

"You are this morning in a good vein, Dido; I wish I could be as merry! My son's absence troubles me not a little, although I seek these ways to put it off, which will not help.

"Care [Worry] that is entered once into the breast

"Will have the whole possession, before it rest."

They exited.

CHAPTER 2
— 2.1 —

Tobias Turf, John Clay, In-and-In Medley, Rasi Clench, To-Pan, D'ogenes Scriben, and Ball Puppy talked together.

Tobias Turf said:

"Zon Clay, cheer up, the better leg avore."

A proverb states, "Set the best foot forward."

He continued:

"This is a veat that is once done, and no more."

The feat was a wedding.

Clench said, "And then it is done vorever, as they say."

A proverb states, "The thing done has an end."

"Right!" Medley said. "Vor a man ha' his hour, and a dog his day."

Two proverbs state, "Every man has his hour," and "Every dog has his day."

Both proverbs mean: Every person will have a successful moment.

Tobias Turf replied, "True, neighbor Medley, you are still In-and-In."

Medley said to himself, "I would be Master Constable, if 'ch [I] could win."

Yes, he would like a promotion to Chief Constable and take the place of Tobias Turf.

To-Pan said:

"I zay, John Clay, keep still on his old gait [chosen path, chosen course].

"Wedding and hanging both go at a rate [the same pace]."

A proverb stated, "Wedding and hanging go by destiny."

Tobias Turf said:

"Well said, To-Pan. You have still the hap — the good fortune — to hit the nail of the head at a close."

A close is a conclusion or a termination.

A proverb states, "Hit the nail on the head."

Tobias Turf continued:

"I think there never was a marriage managed with a more advisement [deliberation] than was this marriage, although I say it who should not say it. Especially 'gain' [against] my own flesh and blood: my wedded wife.

"Indeed, my wife would have had all the young bachelors and maidens, indeed, of the zix parishes hereabout. But I cried, 'None, sweet Sybil, none of that gear [business], I.' It would lick zalt, I told her, by her leave."

"Salt" can mean "lasciviousness." All the young bachelors and maidens would be courting each other.

Tobias Turf continued:

"No, three or vour [four] of our wise, choice, honest neighbors, upstantial [substantial] persons, men who have borne office, and my own family would be enough to eat our dinner.

"What! Dear meat's a thief. I know it by the butchers and the market-volk."

In other words, expensive food is a thief. He did not want to pay an excessive amount of money for food.

Tobias Turf continued:

"Humdrum, I cry."

He wanted a wedding feast that was humdrum and simple, not fancy.

Tobias Turf continued:

"No half ox in a pie. A man that's invited to a bride-ale, if he has cake and drink enough, he need not vear his stake."

A man with enough cake and ale will get a good return on his investment of coming to the wedding and giving a wedding gift.

Clench said, "That is right; he has spoken as true as a gun, believe it."

Dame Sybil Turf, Audrey Turf, and six maids entered the scene. The maids were extra wedding guests.

Tobias Turf said:

"Come, Sybil, come; didn't I tell you about this? Didn't I tell you that this pride and muster — vanity and gathering — of women would mar all? Six women to one daughter, and a mother!

"The Queen — God save her — has no more herself."

Queen Elizabeth I, who never married, had no children. Neither did Queen Mary I, although she did marry. Both queens had more than six serving-women.

Dame Turf said, "Why, if you keep so many maidens as servants, Master Turf, why shouldn't all present our service and show our respects to her?"

Tobias Turf said:

"Your service? Good! I think you'll write 'your very loving and obedient mother' to her shortly.

"Come, send your maids off; I will have them sent home again, wife. I love no trains of Kent or Christendom, as they say."

A train can be a tail. Thomas à Becket was said to have fixed tails to the breeches of men of Kent because one of them cut off Thomas' horse's tail.

A train can also be an entourage.

Joyce, one of the maids, said, "We will not go back and leave our dame."

Madge, another of the maids, said, "Why should Her Worship lack her tail of maids more than you do of men?"

"What? Are you mutinying, Madge?" Tobias Turf asked.

Joan said, "Zend back your c'lons [colons, aka clowns] agen [again], and we will vollow."

"Else we'll guard our dame," all the maids said.

"I ha' zet the nest of wasps all on a flame," Tobias Turf said.

The maids were buzzing angrily.

Dame Turf said:

"Come, you are such another, Master Turf."

"You are such another" means "You are just as bad as they are."

Dame Turf continued:

"A clod you should be called, of a High Constable, to let no music go before your child to church, to cheer her heart up this cold morning!"

Tobias Turf said:

"You are for Father Rosin and his consort [company] of fiddling boys, the great feats [skills] and the less, bycause [for the reason, because] you have entertained [hired] them all from Highgate.

"To show your pomp you'd have your daughter and maids dance over the fields like fays [fairies], to church [in] this frost?"

February is a frosty month.

Tobias Turf said:

"I'll have no roundels [round dances], I, in the queen's paths.

"Let 'un [them] scrape the gut at home, where they have filled it, at afternoon."

The musicians could scrape their catgut — play their strings — in the afternoon, at the Turfs' home.

"I'll have them play at dinner," Dame Turf said.

Clench said, "She is in the right, sir, vor your wedding-dinner is starved without the music."

"If the pies do not come in piping hot, you have lost that proverb," Medley said.

"Piping hot" means "very hot," as in "so hot it makes a piping — hissing — sound."

Some kinds of music-making involve pipes.

"I yield to truth," Tobias Turf said. "Wife, are you sissified [satisfied]?"

"A right good man!" To-Pan said. "When he knows right, he loves it."

Scriben said, "And he will know it and show it, too, by his place of being High Constable, if nowhere else."

Basket Hilts, who was bearded, carried a sword and a dagger. Ball Puppy carried a walking-stick made out of ash-wood; it could be used as a weapon.

Basket Hilts, the serving-man of Squire Tub, was also carrying out part of a plot to get Audrey Turf to marry Squire Tub.

"Well overtaken, gentlemen!" Basket Hilts said. "Please, which man among you is the queen's high constable?"

"The tallest man," Ball Puppy said. "Who else should he be, do you think?"

The tallest man is 1) the greatest in height, and/or 2) the bravest.

"It is no matter what I think, young clown," Basket Hilts said. "Your answer savors of the cart. It is worthy only of a yokel."

Criminals were sometimes paraded in public on a cart.

"What! Cart? And clown?" Ball Puppy said. "Do you know whose team you are speaking to?"

"Team" is a word that applies to cart-horses as well as to people.

Ball Puppy worked for the High Constable.

"No, nor do I care," Basket Hilts said. "Whose jade may you be?"

A jade is an inferior horse.

"Jade? Cart? And clown?" Ball Puppy said. "Oh, for a lash of whipcord! Three-knotted cord!"

Whipcord was used for whips; the knots in the cord would sharpen the pain dealt by the whip.

Basket Hilts said:

"Do you mutter? Sir, snarl this way so that I may hear you, and answer for what you say with my school dagger about your costard, sir."

A costard is 1) literally, an apple, or 2) metaphorically, a head.

His dagger was a school dagger because he would use it to teach Ball Puppy some manners.

Basket Hilts continued:

"Look to it, young grouse. I'll lay it on, and sure.

"Take it off who's wull. [Let whoever is well and willing to try to stop me.]"

He was threatening to beat anyone who interfered with him.

Clench said, "Nay, please, gentleman —"

Basket Hilts interrupted, "Go to, I will not bate him an ace [small part] of it."

The phrase "go to" is often used in "go to Hell."

He began to draw his dagger and said, "What? Roly-poly [Rascal]? Maple [Mottled like maple wood] face? All fellows? [Are all of you cowards?]"

Ball Puppy said:

"Do you hear me, friend?

"I'd wish for you, vor your own good, to tie up your brended [brindled, aka variegated] bitch [sword] there, your dun-colored, rusty, pannier-hilt poinard [basket-hilted dagger], and not vex the young people with showing the teeth of it.

"We now are going to church in way of matrimony, some of us. Th'a' rung all in a'ready. [They have rung the bell that announces that all is ready.]

"If they had not already rung the bell, all the horn-beasts [cattle] that are grazing in this close [enclosed field] should not have pulled me away from here, until this ash-plant [walking-stick] had rung noon on your pate, Master Broom-beard."

Ball Puppy was saying that he would hit Hilts on the head twelve times with his walking-stick if he [Ball Puppy] didn't have a wedding to go to.

"Rung noon" also refers to a cook's custom on knocking on something to announce that the noon meal was ready.

Basket Hilts replied, "That would I fain zee [like to see], quoth [said] the blind George of Holloway. Come, sir!"

He drew his sword and dagger.

"Oh, their naked weapons!" Audrey exclaimed.

The word "weapon" was sometimes used to mean "penis."

"For the passion of man, stop, gentleman and Puppy!" To-Pan said.

"Murder! Oh, murder!" John Clay shouted.

"Oh, my father and mother!" Audrey shouted.

"Husband, what do you mean?" Dame Turf said. "Why aren't you stopping this fight? Son Clay, for God's sake —"

"I charge you in the queen's name, keep the peace," Tobias Turf, the High Constable, said.

"Tell me about no queen or kaiser," Basket Hilts said. "I must have a leg or a haunch of him before I go."

A proverb stated, "He fears nor [neither] king nor kaiser [emperor]."

Medley objected, "But, zir, you must obey the queen's high officers."

"Why must I, goodman Must?" Basket Hilts asked.

"You must, an' you wull," Medley said.

"An'" can mean "and" or "if."

"Wull" can mean "will" or "would."

Tobias Turf said, "Gentleman, I'm here for fault, High Constable. I am here for lack of better circumstances —"

Basket Hilts interrupted, "Are you zo! What then?"

Tobias Turf said, "Please, sir, put up your weapons; do, at my request. As for him — Puppy — on my authority, he shall lie by the heels with his feet in the stocks, *verbatim continente*, an' [if] I live."

He meant by the Latin word *verbatim* "by my words" or "I say." The Latin word *continente* means "continent." He probably meant to say *continenter*, which means "continuously."

The stocks were pieces of wood with half-circles carved out of one edge; when two pieces of wood were put together, the half-circles would form circles. A person would be restrained by having his or her feet put in the circles. The stocks would restrain Ball Puppy's freedom of movement.

Dame Turf said, "Out on him for a knave! What a dead fright he has put me into! Come, Audrey, do not shake."

"But isn't Puppy hurt?" Audrey asked. "Or is the other man hurt?"

"No, bun," John Clay said, "but if I had not cried 'murder,' I wusse [I know] —"

"Bun" is a term of endearment, like "sweetheart."

Ball Puppy interrupted:

"Sweet goodman Clench, I pray you revise [malapropism for 'advise'] my master I may not zit in the stocks until the wedding is over.

"Otherwise, Dame Turf and Mistress Audrey, I shall break the bride-cake."

Ball Puppy was supposed to carry the wedding-cake in the procession.

He was unlikely to drop the wedding-cake and break it on purpose, so he may have meant that he would take a piece of the cake with him so he could eat it while he was in the stocks.

Clench said, "Zomething must be to save authority, Puppy."

Something had to be done to preserve the status of the High Constable: Tobias Turf.

That thing could be to put Ball Puppy in the stocks immediately.

Dame Turf began, "Husband —"

Clench began, "And gossip [friend] —"

Audrey began, "Father —"

Tobias Turf interrupted, "'Treat [Entreat] me not. It is in vain. If he does not lie by the heels, I'll lie there for 'hun [him]; I'll teach the hine [hind = servant] to carry a tongue in his head to his subperiors."

A proverb stated, "Keep a civil tongue in one's head."

"Subperiors" are superiors (who in fact may not be superior).

"This is a wise constable!" Basket Hilts said. "Where does he keep school? Where does he live?"

"In Kentish Town," Clench said. "He is a very survere [severe] man."

Basket Hilts said:

"But, as survere as he is, let me, sir, tell him, he shall not lay his man by the heels [put his serving-man in the stocks] for this.

"This was my quarrel; and by his office leave, if it carry 'hun [him] for this, it shall carry double, vor he shall carry me, too."

In other words, if Tobias Turf puts Puppy in the stocks, he will have to put him [Basket Hilts] in the stocks, too, for they are guilty of the same offense.

"By the breath of man!" Tobias Turf said. "He is my chattel [property], my own hired goods, and if you do abet 'un [aid and encourage him] in this matter, I'll clap you both by the heels, ankle to ankle."

Basket Hilts said:

"You'll clap a dog of wax as soon, old Blurt!"

A "man of wax" may be a man who is having a fit of anger. According to the *Oxford English Dictionary*, one meaning of "wax" is "angry feeling; a fit of anger." "Wax" mainly means this in the expression "to be in a wax."

"Man of wax," however, can be used to emphatically praise a man. It may mean that a man is as handsome as a statue or that a particular man is a man of growth. The man may have grown literally or metaphorically.

One meaning of "dog" is a metal rest placed on either side of a fireplace to support burning wood. A dog made of wax would be useless.

Being called "old Blurt" is an insult.

Basket Hilts continued:

"Come, don't spare me, sir; I am no man's wife — treat me as a man!

"I don't care, I, sir, three skips of a louse for you, and I would not if you were ten tall — brave — constables, not I."

"Nay, please, sir, don't be angry, but content," Tobias Turf said. "My man [employee: Ball Puppy] shall make you what amends you'll ask 'hun [him]."

Basket Hilts said, "Let 'hun mend his manners then, and know his betters. It's all I ask 'hun [of him]; and it will be his own, and his master's, too, another day. 'Che vore 'hun. [I assure him.]"

A proverb stated, "Let him mind his manners; it will be his own another day." In other words: "Let him mind his manners; it will be to his advantage in the long run."

Basket Hilts did not want Ball Puppy to be put in the stocks.

Medley said, "As right as a club, still! Zure [To be sure,] this angry man speaks very near the mark when he is pleased."

"As right as a club" may mean "Might makes right."

"I thank you, sir," Ball Puppy said. "If I meet you at Kentish Town, I will have the courtesy of the hundred for you."

In other words, Ball Puppy would buy Basket Hilts a drink should they meet in Kentish Town.

Basket Hilts said:

"Gramercy [Thank you], good High Constable's hine [hind = servant]!

"But do you hear me?

"Mas' [Master] Constable, I have other manner of matter to bring you about than this. And so it is: I do belong to [am a retainer of] one of the queen's captains, a gentleman of the battlefield, one Captain Thumbs.

"I don't know whether you know 'hun [him] or not. It may be you do, and it may be you do not again."

"No," Tobias Turf said. "I assure you on my constableship that I do not know 'hun [him].

Basket Hilts said to himself, "Nor do I know him, either, indeed."

There was no Captain Thumbs to know. As would soon become apparent, Captain Thumbs would be Chanon Hugh in disguise.

Basket Hilts said out loud:

"It skills — matters — not much.

"My captain and myself, having occasion to come riding by here, this morning, at the corner of St. John's Wood some miles west of this town, were set upon by a group of country fellows, who not only beat us but robbed us most sufficiently and efficiently, and bound us to restrain our behavior, hand and foot; and so they left us.

"Now, Don [a complimentary title] Constable, I am to charge you in Her Majesty's name, as you will answer it at your apperil [peril], that forthwith you raise a hue and cry in the hundred, for all such persons as you can dispect [suspect], by the length and breadth of your office.

"Vor I tell you the loss is of some value; therefore, look to it."

The words "hue" and "cry" both mean "outcry." The law officers were obliged to raise a hue and cry of citizens pursuing criminals. If they did not, the borough would be obliged to compensate the victim. In Ben Jonson's play, the High Constable is responsible for making the payment.

Tobias Turf said:

"As fortune mend me now, or any office of a thousand pounds, if I know what to zay."

He didn't know what to say, and he still wouldn't know what to say even if he should have good fortune or an appointment worth a thousand pounds.

This emergency was coming at a bad time: This was the wedding day of his daughter.

Tobias Turf continued:

"I wish that I were dead or vair hanged up at Tyburn, that place of capital punishment, if I do know what course to take, or how [which way] to turn myself.

"Just at this time, too, now, my daughter is to be married!

"I'll just go to Pancridge church nearby, and return instantly, and all my neighborhood shall go about the hue and cry."

He would see John Clay and Audrey married, and then he would return and lead the hue and cry.

Basket Hilts' goal was to have Audrey Turf marry someone else. Because he did not want the marriage to John Clay to happen, he said:

"Tut, Pancridge me no Pancridge! Don't try to get out of your duty! If you let it slip, you will answer for it, and your cap will be made out of wool."

By law, lower-class men wore wool caps. If Tobias Turf did not do his duty, he could lose his job and status.

Basket Hilts continued:

"Therefore take heed, you'll feel the smart else, Constable."

Tobias Turf replied, "Nay, good sir, stay."

He then asked, "Neighbors, what do you think about this?"

His wife, Dame Turf, began, "Indeed, man —"

Tobias Turf said:

"By God's precious blood, woman, hold your tongue, and mind your pigs on the spit at home; you must have your oar in everything."

He then asked Basket Hilts, "Please, sir, what kind of fellows were they?"

Basket Hilts answered, "Thieves' kind, I have told you."

"I mean, what kind of men?" Tobias Turf replied.

"Men of our make and kind," Basket Hilts said.

Tobias Turf responded:

"Nay, but with patience, sir, we who are officers must inquire about the special marks, and all the tokens of the despected [suspected] parties, or perhaps, else, we will be never the near [nearer] of our purpose in apprehending them.

"Can you tell what apparel any of them wore?"

Basket Hilts said:

"In truth, no; there were so many o'hun [of them], all similar to each another."

Basket Hilts then described the leader of the robbers as looking exactly like John Clay:

"Now I remember that there was one busy fellow who was their leader.

"He was a blunt, squat swad [stupid, thickset bumpkin], but lower [shorter] than yourself.

"He had on a leather doublet with long points, and a pair of pinned-up breeches, like pudding-bags, with yellow stockings, and his hat turned up with a silver clasp, on his leer [left] side."

Dame Turf said, "Judging by these marks, the leader of the robbers should be John Clay, now bless the man!"

"Peace, and be naught [be quiet]!" Tobias Turf said. "I think the woman be in a frenzic [frenzy]."

"John Clay?" Basket Hilts said. "Who's he, good mistress?"

Audrey said, "He is the man who shall be my husband "

"What!" Basket Hilts said. "Your husband, pretty one?"

Audrey said, "Yes, I shall soon be married."

She pointed to John Clay and said, "That's he."

Tobias Turf said, "Passion of me, I am undone! I am ruined!"

He thought that John Clay, his son-in-law-to-be, was a robber.

"Bless master's son!" Ball Puppy said.

Basket Hilts said to John Clay, "Oh, you are well apprehended. Do you know — recognize — me, sir?"

"No's my record [answer]," John Clay said. "I never zaw you avore [before]."

"You did not?" Basket Hilts said. "Where were your eyes then? Out at washing?"

If the eyes were too dirty to see with, they must have needed a wash.

Tobias Turf said:

"What should a man zay? Who should he trust in these days?"

"Listen, John Clay, if you have done any such thing, tell the truth and shame the devil."

"In faith, do that," Clench said. "My gossip [friend] Turf zays well to you, John."

"Speak, man," Medley said, "but do not convess, nor be avraid."

Instead of "confess," Medley may have meant to say, "hold back."

To-Pan said, "A man is a man, and a beast's a beast, look to it."

In other words, act like a man, not like a beast.

Dame Turf said:

"In the name of men or beasts, what are you doing?

"Hare [Harry] the poor fellow out of his five wits, and seven senses?"

In Shakespeare's time, people were believed to have five wits: memory, fantasy, judgment, imagination, and common sense.

The traditional five senses are hearing, sight, touch, taste, and smell.

The others all seemed to think that John Clay was guilty of robbery.

Dame Turf comforted him:

"Do not weep, John Clay."

She then said to all the others:

"I swear the poor wretch is as guilty from [of] it as the child is who was born this very morning."

She meant that he was as innocent of committing robbery as was a newly born child.

John Clay said:

"No, as I am a kyrsin [Christian] soul, I wish I were hanged if ever I —

"Alas! I wish I were out of my life so I wish I were, and in again —"

He was very upset, and he was wishing that he were dead if he had committed robbery.

Ball Puppy said:

"Nay, Mistress Audrey will say nay to that.

"No in-and-out? If you were out of your life, what should she do for a husband? Who should fall aboard of her then? [Who should mount her then?]"

If John Clay were dead, Audrey would not like it because she would have no in-and-out (sex) and she would have no husband.

Ball Puppy then said to himself:

"Ball? He's a puppy!

"No, Hannibal has no breeding!"

Ball Puppy was of a low social class, and he had no wife with whom to have sex. And Audrey would be likely to reject him if he asked her to marry him.

He then said out loud:

"Well, I say little."

A proverb stated, "Though he say little, he thinks much."

He continued:

"But hitherto all goes well — pray it prove no better."

He probably meant to say: But so far all goes well — let's hope the future proves to be no worse."

"Come, father; I wish we — John Clay and I — were married!" Audrey said. "I am a-cold."

Valentine's Day was cold, but a husband would warm her up.

Basket Hilts said:

"Well, Master Constable, this your fine groom [a groom can be a servant] here, bridegroom, or whatsoever groom else he is, I charge him with the felony, and I order you to carry him back forthwith to the village of Paddington to my captain, who awaits my return there.

"I am to go to the next justice of peace, to get a warrant to raise a hue and cry and bring him and his fellows all afore 'hun [before him].

"Fare you well, sir, and look to 'hun [him] and keep him secure, I charge you, as you'll answer it.

"Take heed; the business, if you defer it, may prejudicial [injure] you more than you think for [more than you expect].

"Zay [Say] I told you so."

Basket Hilts exited.

Tobias Turf said:

"Here's a bride-ale indeed!

"Ah, zon John, zon Clay! I little thought you would have proved a piece — a coin — of such false metal."

And false mettle.

John Clay replied to his prospective father-in-law:

"Father, will you believe me?

"I wish I might never stir in my new shoes if ever I would do so voul a fact [so foul an evil deed]."

Tobias Turf said:

"Well, neighbors, I do order you to assist me with taking 'hun [him] to Paddington.

"If he is a true man, good; all the better for 'hun [him].

"I will do my duty, even if he were my own begotten son a thousand times."

Dame Turf said, "Why, do you hear me, man? Husband? Master Turf?"

He ignored her and exited with Clench, Medley, To-Pan, and Scriben, and with John Clay in his custody.

Dame Turf said:

"What shall my daughter do?

"Puppy, stay here."

In this society, young women such as Audrey were accompanied by male protectors or by chaperones.

Dame Turf followed her husband and neighbors. Her maids went with her, leaving Audrey Turf and Ball Puppy behind.

Audrey said, "Mother, I'll go with you and with my father."

Ball Puppy said, "Nay, stay, sweet Mistress Audrey. Here are none but one friend — as they zay — who desires to speak a word or two, cold, with you."

A proverb stated, "Here are none but friends."

The words were "cold" because they were unexpected by Audrey. They were also spoken in cold weather.

"How do you veel yourself this frosty morning?" Ball Puppy asked.

Audrey replied, "What have you to do to ask, I ask you? [Why do you ask?] I am a-cold."

The word "cold" can mean "without passion." Puppy wanted her to be passionate.

Ball Puppy touched her hand and said, "It seems you are hot, good Mistress Audrey."

"You lie," Audrey said, slapping his hand away. "I am as cold as ice is. Feel someone or something else."

"Nay, you have cooled my courage," Ball Puppy said. "I am past it. I have done feeling with you."

"Courage" can mean 1) "valor," or 2) "desire for sex."

The word "do" can mean "have sex with."

"Done with me! [Had sex with me!]" Audrey said. "I do defy you, so I do, to say you have done with me. You are a saucy Puppy."

"Oh, you mistake my meaning!" Ball Puppy said. "I meant not as you think I meant."

"Meant you not knavery, Puppy?" Audrey asked.

"No, not I," Ball Puppy said. "Clay meant you all the knavery, it seems, who, rather than he would be married to you, chose to be wedded to the gallows first."

Many criminals, including robbers, such as John Clay was accused of being, were hung.

"I thought he was a dissembler," Audrey said. "I thought that he would prove to be a slippery merchant in the frost. He might have married one first, and have been hanged after, if he had had a mind to it. But you men — bah!"

Ball Puppy asked, "Mistress Audrey, can you vind [find] in your heart to fancy Puppy? Me, poor Ball?"

Audrey said, "You are disposed to jeer at and mock one, Master Hannibal."

Basket Hilts entered the scene.

Seeing him, Audrey said, "Have pity on me — it's the angry man with the beard!"

Ball Puppy took off his hat.

Basket Hilts said to Ball Puppy, "Put on thy hat, I look for no despect."

"Despect" sounds like "des'spect," aka "disrespect," and it means "looking-down-on," but Basket Hilts meant that he was looking for no marks of respect.

"Where's thy master?" Basket Hilts asked Ball Puppy.

"By the Virgin Mary, he has gone with the picture of despair to Paddington," Ball Puppy replied.

The picture of despair was John Clay.

Basket Hilts said:

"Please run after 'hun [him] and tell 'hun he shall find my captain lodged at the Red Lion in Paddington; that's the inn.

"Let 'un [him] ask vor Captain Thumbs. And take that for thy pains."

He gave Ball Puppy some money and said, "He may seek long enough else."

In other words: Otherwise, he may look for him for a long time.

Basket Hilts said, "Hie thee again."

In other words: Hurry back.

"Yes, sir," Ball Puppy said. "You'll look to [after] Mistress Bride the while?"

"That I will," Basket Hilts said. "Please hurry."

Ball Puppy exited.

"What, Puppy!" Audrey said. "Puppy!"

He was leaving her with the angry bearded man.

"Sweet Mistress Bride, he'll come again very soon," Basket Hilts said.

He said ironically to himself:

"Here was no subtle device to get a wench. This Chanon has a brave pate [head] of his own! A shaven pate, and a right monger, i' vaith!"

Chanon Hugh was a priest, and he had a shaven tonsure; still, he was a right monger — a disreputable dealer or trader — and possibly a whoremonger.

Basket Hilts continued talking to himself:

"This was his plot!

"I follow Captain Thumbs? We robbed in St. John's Wood? In my other hose! [Pull my other leg!] I laugh to think what a fine fool's finger they have of this wise constable, in pricking — pointing — out this Captain Thumbs to his neighbors."

The "fool's finger" is the middle finger, which is pointed at fools.

Basket Hilts continued talking to himself:

"You shall see the tile-man, too, set fire on his own kiln, and leap into it to save himself from hanging."

The tile-man is John Clay.

Basket Hilts continued talking to himself:

"You talk of a bride-ale? Here was a bride-ale broke in the nick!"

The words "pricking" and "nick" have bawdy meanings. A "nick" is a notch or indentation. Bawdily, a prick can fit in a nick. Of course, "nick" can also mean "nick of time."

Basket Hilts continued talking to himself:

"Well, I must yet dispatch this bride to my own master, the young Squire, and then my task is done."

He said out loud to Audrey:

"Gentlewoman, I have in some sort done you some wrong, but now I'll do you what right I can.

"It's true you are a proper woman, but to be cast away on such a clown-pipe as Clay!"

A pipe can be 1) a wind instrument, or 2) a container for holding liquids.

John Clay is a clown-pipe or rustic-pipe. He is a rural fellow and may be talkative and have a beer belly.

Basket Hilts continued talking to Audrey:

"I think that your friends are not as wise as nature might have made them.

"Well, go to; there's better fortune coming toward you, if you do not deject and regret it. Take a vool's counsel" — as many characters in this play do, Basket Hilts unintentionally said the opposite of what he meant; he was unlikely to consider himself a fool — "and do not stand in your own light and undersell yourself.

"It may prove to be better than you expect, you will see."

Audrey asked, "Alas, sir, what is it you would have me do? I'd fain — eagerly — do all for the best, if I knew how."

Basket Hilts replied, "Don't forsake a good turn when it is offered to you, fair mistress Audrey — that's your name, I take it?"

"I am no Mistress, sir. My name is Audrey."

She was no Mistress — "Mistress" was a polite title for a female head of household, and Audrey was still not married. She, however, was a woman whom men loved and so she was a mistress in that (nonsexual) sense.

Basket Hilts said, "Well, it so happens that there is a bold young squire, the blood — lively aristocratic man — of Totten Court, Tub, and Tripoly —"

"Squire Tub, you mean," Audrey said. "I know him; he knows me, too."

"He is in love with you; and more, he's mad for you," Basket Hilts said.

"Aye, so he told me — he is in his wits, I think," Audrey said. "But he's too fine for me, and he has a Lady Tub as his mother."

"Lady" was a higher title than "Squire."

Squire Tub entered the scene.

Seeing him, Audrey said, "Here he comes himself!"

"Oh, you are a trusty governor!" Squire Tub said to Basket Hilts.

"What ails you?" Basket Hilts said. "You do not know when you're well, I think. You'd have the calf with the white face, sir, would you? I have her for you here; what more do you want?"

A calf with a white face is a pretty calf or a pretty fool.

"Quietness, Hilts, and I would hear no more of it," Squire Tub said.

"No more of it, do you say?" Basket Hilts said. "I do not care if some of us had not heard so much of it, I tell you truly. A man must carry and vetch like Bungy's dog for you."

Friar Bungay was a magician; the familiar spirits of magicians had the form of animals.

Squire Tub asked, "What's he?"

Basket Hilts answered:

"A spaniel — and scarcely be spit in the mouth for it."

In this society, people believed that dogs liked to be spit in the mouth and so it was a sign of approval.

Basket Hilts continued:

"A good dog deserves, sir, a good bone, from a free — generous — master.

"But, if your turns are served and you have gotten what you needed, the devil a bit — not at all — you care for a man after, ever a lard — lord — of you.

"'Like will to like, indeed,' quoth the scabbed squire to the mangy knight, when both met in a dish of buttered vish."

A proverb stated, "A scabbed horse is good enough for a scabbed squire."

Normally, a squire and a knight might meet *over* a dish of buttered fish while sharing a meal.

Basket Hilts continued:

"One bad, there's never a good —"

A proverb stated, "One bad, the other worse."

Another proverb stated, "One bad apple spoils the barrel."

Basket Hilts continued:

"— and not a barrel better herring among you."

In other words: You lords and masters are all alike — bad.

Squire Tub said:

"Nay, Hilts, please, don't grow frampold [peevish and disagreeable] now.

"Turn not the bad cow after thy good sope [draught]."

A proverb stated that "a curst cow gives a good pail of milk but throws it down with her heels." That is, a cursed cow gives a good pail of milk but then kicks it over with her hoof.

In other words: You have done something good; don't ruin it now by doing something bad.

Squire Tub continued:

"Our plot has hitherto taken good effect; and should it now be troubled or stopped up, it would prove to be the utter ruin of my hopes.

"I ask thee to hasten to Pancridge, to the Chanon [Chanon Hugh], and give him notice of our good success. Tell him to make all things in readiness.

"Pretty Audrey and myself will cross the fields, using the nearest path.

"Good Hilts, make thou some haste, and meet us on the way."

He then said, "Come, gentle Audrey."

Basket Hilts said:

"Vaith, I wish I had a few more geances for it!"

The word "geances" may mean 1) a rustic pronunciation of "chances," 2) a rustic pronunciation of lira "genovese," aka small Genovese coins, or 2) "'geances," aka acts of vengeance.

The best answer is probably that he would like a reward for his work: some coins.

Basket Hilts continued:

"If you say the word, send me to Jericho.

"Outcept [Unless] a man were a post-horse, I have not known the like of it; yet if he had kind words, it would never irk 'hun [him].

"But a man may break his heart out in these days and get a flap with a foxtail when he has done.

"And there is all!"

The idiom "get a flap with a foxtail" means "be scorned for his efforts."

Squire Tub said:

"No, don't say that, Hilts."

He gave him some money and said:

"Wait a moment, there are crowns [coins] — my love and respect for you bestows them on thee for thy reward.

"If gold will please thee, all my land shall drop in bounty thus, to recompense thy merit."

Basket Hilts said:

"Tut, keep your land and your gold, too, sir. I seek neither-nother [neither] of 'hun [them]. Learn to get more: You will know to spend that zum you have early enough.

"You are assured of me. I love you too, too well to live on the spoil of you — money plundered from you.

"For your own sake, I wish that there were no worse than I!

"All is not gold that glisters [glistens].

"I'll go to Pancridge."

Filled with emotion, he exited, weeping.

Squire Tub said:

"See how his love does melt him into tears! An honest, faithful servant is a jewel.

"Now the adventurous Squire has time and leisure to ask his Audrey how she is doing, and to hear a grateful answer from her."

He waited a moment, and then he said:

"She does not speak.

"Has the proud tyrant, frost, usurped the seat of former beauty in my love's fair cheek, staining the roseate tincture of her blood with the dull dye of blue-congealing cold?

"No, surely the weather dares not so presume to hurt an object of her brightness.

"Yet the more I view her, she but looks so, so.

"Ha! Give me leave — permission — to search this mystery!

"Oh, now I have it."

He said to Audrey, "Bride, I know your grief. The last night's cold has bred in you such horror of the assigned bridegroom's constitution, the Kilburn claypit — that frost-bitten marl [fertilizer], that lump in courage, melting cake of ice — that the conceit [understanding] thereof has almost killed thee.

"But I must do thee good, wench, and refresh thee."

He was saying that she was upset because she had discovered that John Clay was a robber.

"You are a merry man, Squire Tub of Totten Court!" Audrey said. "I have heard much of your words, but not of your deeds."

"Thou say the truth, sweet," Squire Tub said. "I have been too slack in deeds."

"Yet I was never so strait-laced — so grudging — to you, Squire," Audrey said.

"Why, did you ever love me, gentle Audrey?" Squire Tub asked.

"Love you? I cannot tell," Audrey said. "I must hate nobody, my father says."

"Yes, Clay and Kilburn," Squire Tub said. "Audrey, you must hate them."

If she married him, she would have to hate John Clay and the village from which he came: Kilburn.

"It shall be for your sake then," Audrey said.

To love a higher-class man such as Squire Tub, she believed that she would have to hate some lower-class people and places.

"And 'for my sake' shall yield you that gratuity," Squire Tub said.

The "gratuity" was meant to be a kiss.

He attempted to kiss her, but she pushed him back.

"Soft and fair, Squire," Audrey said. "There go two words to a bargain."

In this context, "soft and fair" meant "not so fast." She wanted to be treated soft and fair: gently and fairly and with respect.

"What are those two words, Audrey?" Squire Tub asked.

"Soft and fair" can mean "gentle and beautiful."

Audrey could bring these qualities to a marriage to Squire Tub that would give her a rise in social status.

"Nay, I cannot tell," Audrey said. "My mother said, zure [to be sure], if you married me, you'd make me a lady the first week, and put me in I know not what, the very day."

He would make her a lady, and he would do a second thing.

"What was it?" Squire Tub asked about the second thing. "Speak, gentle Audrey, thou shall have it yet."

Audrey answered:

"A velvet dressing for my head is, they say, something that will make one brave — splendid.

"I will not know Bess Moale nor Margery Turnup; I will look another way upon them, and I will be proud."

"Moale" may mean "mo' ale" or "more ale," and "Turnup" is similar to "Turnip." "Moale" can also mean "mole." "Turnup" can also mean "turn up," as in an upturned nose. Food that turns one's stomach is food that the stomach rejects and revolts against.

She would no longer be friends with her friends because of her rise in society. She would look down on them.

Marriage to Squire Tub would put her in fine clothing and would put her in a position where, she thought, she would have to look down on her friends.

Squire Tub said to himself:

"Truly, I could wish my wench a better wit. I could wish that she were more intelligent."

Possibly, they were not communicating. Possibly, Audrey believed that if she became Squire Tub's wife, he would want her to become proud and look down on her friends. But possibly, Squire Tub wanted her to hate her former beau, John Clay, but not to look down on her friends, After all, he had shown sensitivity to Basket Hilts' feelings.

But possibly, Audrey did not want to be proud. Possibly, she was resisting marriage with Squire Tub, whom she believed was too socially high-ranking for her.

Squire Tub continued speaking to himself:

"But what she lacks in intelligence, her face supplies — makes up for.

"There is a sharply pointed luster — beauty — in her eye that has shot quite through me and has hit my heart, and thence it is I first received the wound that rankles and festers now, which only she can cure.

"Eagerly would I escape from this state of mind, but, being flesh, I cannot. I must love her, the naked truth is; and I will go on, were it for nothing but to cross my rivals."

He then said out loud:

"Come, Audrey, I am now resolved to have thee."

He wanted her to be his wife.

Justice Preamble and Miles Metaphor entered the scene.

Miles Metaphor was dressed as a pursuivant, a royal messenger. A pursuivant-at-arms has the legal authority to make arrests.

"Do it quickly, Miles," Justice Preamble said. "Why do thou shake, man? Just speak his name; I'll second thee myself."

Justice Preamble was saying that Miles Metaphor need only speak the name of the man he was "arresting." Justice Preamble would do what else needed to be done.

"What is his name?" Miles Metaphor asked.

"Squire Tripoly, or Tub," Justice Preamble said. "Anything —"

They walked over to Squire Tub.

Miles Metaphor said, "Squire Tub, I arrest you in the queen's majesty's name, and the name of all the Privy Council's."

"Arrest me, varlet?" Squire Tub said.

"Keep the peace, I order you," Justice Preamble said.

"Are you there, Justice Bramble?" Squire Tub asked. "Where's your warrant?"

Justice Preamble answered, "The warrant is directed here to me, from the whole Privy Council table; wherefore I would ask you to be patient, Squire, and make good the peace."

He had no warrant, so he lied and said that the Privy Council table was sending him one.

Squire Tub replied, "Well, at your pleasure, Justice. I am wronged."

He then asked Miles Metaphor, "Sirrah, who are you who have arrested me?"

"He is a pursuivant-at-arms, Squire Tub," Justice Preamble said.

"I am a pursuivant," Miles Metaphor said. "You can see by my coat."

Miles Metaphor was wearing a pursuivant's distinctive coat.

"Well, pursuivant, go with me," Squire Tub said. "I'll give you bail."

Justice Preamble said:

"Sir, he may take no bail. It is a warrant in special from the Council, and it commands your personal appearance.

"Sir, I must take your weapon and then deliver you as a prisoner to this officer."

He took Squire Tub's sword and said:

"Squire Tub, I ask you to conceive of me no other than as your friend and neighbor.

"Let my person be severed from my office in the deed I am performing here, and I am clear and beyond reproof."

He then said to Miles Metaphor:

"Here, pursuivant, receive him into your hands, and treat him like a gentleman."

"I thank you, sir," Squire Tub said. "But where must I go now?"

Justice Preamble replied:

"Nay, that must not be told you until you come to the place assigned by his instructions.

"I'll be the maiden's convoy — her escort — to her father for this time, Squire."

Squire Tub said:

"I thank you, Master Bramble. I doubt or fear you will make her the balance — the scales of justice — to weigh your justice in. Please, do me right and don't lead her, at least, out of the way.

"Justice is blind, and having a blind guide,

"She may be apt to slip aside."

Squire Tub realized that Justice Preamble wanted to marry Audrey.

"I'll see to her," Justice Preamble said.

"See" means "look after," but in this context it means that Justice Preamble would not be blind justice.

Justice Preamble and Audrey exited.

Squire Tub said:

"I see my wooing will not thrive. Arrested just as I had set my rest up — made a firm decision — for a wife, and being so fair for it, as I was! Everything was working out well!

"Well, Lady Fortune, thou are a blind bawd and a beggar, too, to cross me thus, and let my only rival get her from me! That's the spite of spites."

Whom does Squire Tub regard as his only rival?

His only rival was Justice Preamble, who intended to marry Audrey at Pancridge church.

John Clay was out of the picture because he was suspected of being a robber.

Squire Tub continued:

"But what I most wonder at is that I, being none of the court, am sent for thither by the Council.

"My heart is not as light as it was in the morning."

Basket Hilts entered the scene and said to Squire Tub:

"You mean to make a hoyden — a fool — or a hare of me, to hunt counter thus and to make these doubles."

"Doubles" are sharp turns, sometimes moving back on the course, and "to hunt counter" means to follow the scent of the hunted prey in the wrong direction — away from, not toward, the prey.

He continued:

"And you mean no such thing as you send about — as you said you would do!

"Where's your sweetheart now, I wonder?"

He was wondering why Audrey wasn't present. Basket Hilts had gone to a lot of trouble to get her for his master: Squire Tub.

"Oh, Hilts!" Squire Tub said.

Basket Hilts said:

"I know you of old! Never halt — that is, limp — in front of a cripple. Don't attempt to trick me.

"Will you have a caudle? Where's your grief and pain, sir? Speak."

A caudle is a medicinal drink.

"Do you hear me, friend?" Miles Metaphor said to Basket Hilts. "Do you serve this gentleman?"

"What then, sir? What if I do?" Basket Hilts said. "Peradventure yea, peradventure nay. Maybe I do, and maybe I don't. What's that to you, sir? Speak."

"Nay, please, sir, I meant no harm, in truth," Miles Metaphor said. "But this good gentleman has been arrested."

Angry, Basket Hilts said, "What! Say that to me again."

Squire Tub said, "Nay, Basket, never storm. I am arrested here, upon command from the Queen's Council and I must obey."

"You say, sir, very truly, that you must obey," Miles Metaphor said. "You are an honest gentleman, indeed!"

"He must?" Basket Hilts said.

"But that which most torments me is this: Justice Bramble has taken away from here my Audrey," Squire Tub said.

Basket Hilts said:

"What! What!

"Stand aside a little, sirrah, you with the badge on your breast. Let's know, sir, who and what you are."

Miles Metaphor said, "I am, sir — please, do not look so terribly angry — a pursuivant."

"A pursuivant!" Basket Hilts said. "What is your name, sir?"

Miles Metaphor said, "My name, sir —"

"What is it?" Basket Hilts interrupted. "Speak!"

He answered, "Miles Metaphor, and Justice Preamble's clerk."

Squire Tub asked Basket Hilts, "What does he say?"

Basket Hilts said, "Please, let us alone."

He then asked Miles Metaphor, "You are a pursuivant?"

Afraid, Miles Metaphor answered, "No, indeed, sir, I wish I might never stir from you. I was made a pursuivant against my will."

"Ha!" Basket Hilts said, "And who made you one? Tell the truth, or my will shall make you nothing, instantly."

He drew his sword, and Miles Metaphor fell to his knees.

Miles Metaphor said, "Put up your frightful blade, and your dead-doing — death-dealing — look, and I shall tell you everything."

"Speak then the truth, and the whole truth, and nothing but the truth," Basket Hilts ordered.

Miles Metaphor said:

"My master, Justice Bramble, hearing that your master, the Squire Tub, was coming on this way with Mistress Audrey, the High Constable's daughter, made me a pursuivant and gave me warrant — the authority — to arrest him, so that he might get the lady, with whom he has gone to Pancridge, to the vicar, not to her father's.

"This was the plot, which, I beseek [beseech] you, do not tell my master."

Squire Tub said, "Oh, wonderful! Well, Basket, let him rise."

Miles Metaphor rose.

Squire Tub said to him, "Forge some excuse for my free escape. I'll post — quickly go — to Paddington to acquaint old Tobias Turf with the whole business, and so stop the marriage."

Squire Tub exited.

Basket Hilts said, "Well, bless thee. I wish thee grace to keep thy master's secrets better or be hanged."

Miles Metaphor replied:

"I thank you for your gentle admonition and advice.

"Please, let me call you godfather hereafter."

Godfathers provide spiritual guidance.

He continued:

"And, as your godson Metaphor, I promise to keep my master's privities sealed up in the valise — traveling bag — of my trust, locked close and secret forever, or let me be trussed up at Tyburn shortly."

"Privities" are 1) secrets, and 2) private parts, genitals.

Basket Hilts replied, "May thine own wish save or choke thee! Let's go."

They exited.

CHAPTER 3

— 3.1 —

Tobias Turf, Clench, Medley, To-Pan, Scriben, and John Clay stood together outside Tobias Turf's house.

Tobias Turf said:

"By the passion of me, was any man ever thus crossed? All things run arsy-varsy [topsy-turvy], upside down.

"High Constable! Now by Our Lady of Walsingham, I had rather be marked out as a Tom Scavenger, and with a shovel make clean the highways, than have this office of a constable, and a High Constable!"

Walsingham was a place of pilgrimages.

A scavenger was a street-cleaner.

The job of High Constable was turning out to have a lot of responsibility. Tobias Turf had to make a hue and cry after non-existent robbers, although he did not know that they were non-existent. He also had to arrest John Clay, the man who had been about to marry Audrey, the High Constable's daughter.

Tobias Turf continued:

"The higher the charge, it brings more trouble, more vexation with it."

The greater the job and responsibility, the more the trouble and the vexation it brings with it.

Tobias Turf continued:

"Neighbors, good neighbors, 'vize me [advise me] what to do.

"How shall we bear ourselves in this hue and cry?

"We cannot find the Captain; no such man lodged at the Lion or came thither hurt.

"The morning we have spent in privy search, and because of that the bride-ale is deferred. The bride, she's left alone in Puppy's charge. The bridegroom, John Clay, goes under a pair of sureties — that is, under two people who have stood bail for him — and he is considered by all as a respected person."

John Clay was not locked up because he had been bailed out by two people — including Tobias Turf, as will soon become known — who had guaranteed his presence at the time of trial. Now he was assisting in the hue and cry — the search — for the so-called other robbers.

Earlier, everyone had suspected that John Clay was a robber, but now they were returning to their original opinion that he was worthy of respect. That is why two people had stood surety for him.

Tobias Turf concluded:

"How should we bustle forward? Give me some counsel how to bestir our stumps in these cross ways."

"Stumps" are legs.

Clench said:

"Indeed, gossip Turf, you have, you say, remission [commission] to comprehend [apprehend] all such as are dispected [suspected]."

"Now would I make another privy search through this town, and then you have zearched two towns."

Medley said:

"Masters, take heed, let's not vind too many. One's enough to stay the hangman's stomach."

That is, one criminal is enough to satisfy the hangman's appetite for hanging.

Medley continued:

"There is John Clay, who is yvound [found] already. He is a proper [handsome] man, a tile-man by his trade. He is a man, as one would zay, molded in clay, as spruce and smart in appearance as any neighbor's child among you."

Saying that a man was molded in wax was a compliment. Such a man was a perfect man, one who resembled a statue.

Medley continued:

"And he — you zee — is taken on conspition [suspicion], and two or three — they zay — what call you 'em?

"Zuch as the justices of *coram nobis* [the King's Bench] grant — I forget their names, you have many of them, Master High Constable, they come to you.

"I ha' it at my tongue's end — coney-burrows, to bring him straight avore the zessions house."

Medley was trying to think of the word "warrants"; the word "warrens," meaning a habitat for rabbits, is close to it.

Conies are rabbits, and most species of rabbits burrow into the earth to create homes. A group of coney-burrows is called a warren.

"Oh, you mean warrens [warrants], neighbor, don't you?" Tobias Turf asked.

"Aye, aye, thick same [the very same]! You know 'un [them] well enough," Medley said.

Tobias Turf said:

"Too well, too well; I wish I had never known them!

"We good vreeholders [freeholders] cannot live in quiet, but every hour new purcepts [precepts, orders], hues and cries, put us to requisitions night and day."

A freeholder is a person who owns land and is able to dispose of it at will.

"Requisitions" is possibly a portmanteau word combining "requirements" and "inquisitions." Duties such as raising a hue and cry, however, do requisition and require the High Constable's time.

Tobias Turf continued:

"What should a man zay? Should we leave the zearch?

"If I do, I am in danger [liable] to reburse [reimburse] as much as he was robbed of; aye, and pay his hurts [pay for the damage done to him].

"If I should vollow it [continue the search], all the good cheer — food — that was provided for the wedding dinner will be spoiled and lost. Oh, there are two vat pigs a-zindging [being singed] by the vire [fire], now by Saint Tony, too good to eat except on a wedding-day."

Saint Anthony the Abbot (not Saint Anthony of Padua), aka Saint Anthony of the Desert, is the patron saint of swineherds.

Tobias Turf continued:

"And then there is also being cooked a goose that will bid you all, 'Come cut me!'"

A proverb stated, "Here is a goose so finely roasted it cries, 'Come eat me.'"

Tobias Turf continued:

"Zun Clay, zun Clay — for I must call thee so — be of good comfort; take my muckinder [handkerchief] and dry thine eyes."

John Clay, Tobias Turf's still prospective son-in-law, had been crying.

A possible punishment for robbery was hanging.

Tobias Turf continued:

"If thou are true and honest, and if thou find thy conscience clear vrom [from] it [the robbery you are suspected of committing], pluck up a good heart [cheer up]: We'll do well enough.

"If not, confess, in truth's name.

"But in faith, I dare to be sworn upon all holy books that John Clay would never commit a robbery on his own head."

"On his own head" means 1) against himself (i.e., he would never rob himself), and/or 2) on his own responsibility.

John Clay said:

"No, truth is my rightful judge; I have kept my hands here hence [away] from evil speaking, lying, and slandering, and my tongue from stealing.

"The man does not live this day who can say 'John Clay, I have zeen thee, except in the way of honesty.'"

This meant: All who have seen me, John Clay, have never seen me be dishonest.

To-Pan said, "Indeed, neighbor Medley, I dare to be his borrow [security] that he would not look a true man in the vace."

Of course, if John Clay were honest, he would look a true man in the face.

John Clay said:

"I take the town to concord [agree], where I dwell, all Kilburn be my witness, if I were not begot in bashfulness, brought up in shamefacedness [modesty].

"Let 'un [them] bring a dog but to my vace, that can zay I ha' beat 'hun [him], and without a vault [fault]."

In other words, when John Clay beats a dog, the dog deserves it.

John Clay continued:

"Or but a cat that will swear upon a book I have as much as zet avire [set on fire] her tail, and I'll give him or her a crown for 'mends [amends].

"But to give out and zay I have robbed a captain!

"Receive me at the latter day, if I ever thought of any such matter, or could mind it —"

The latter day is the Day of Judgment. Instead of "Receive me," he meant, "Refuse me," aka "Reject and condemn me."

In-and-In Medley said:

"No, John, you are come of too good personage [family].

"I think my gossip [friend] Clench and Master Turf both think you would attempt no such voul matter."

Tobias Turf said:

"But how unhappily it comes to pass just on the wedding-day!

"I beg your mercy, I had almost forgotten the hue and cry.

"Good neighbor Pan, you are the thirdborough [petty constable], and D'ogenes Scriben, you are my learnèd writer, so make out a new purcept [precept]."

A precept is a writ or warrant. The warrant would be for the men they were pursuing in a hue and cry.

Tobias Turf continued:

"Lord, for thy goodness, I had forgotten my daughter all this while!

"The idle knave has brought no news from her."

Seeing Ball Puppy coming, he said:

"Here comes the sneaking Puppy.

"What's the news? My heart! My heart! I fear all is not well. Something's misshaped [mis-happed, gone wrong] since he has come without Audrey."

Ball Puppy and Dame Turf entered the scene.

Ball Puppy said, "Oh, where's my master? My master! My master!"

Dame Turf said, "Thy master! What would thou want with thy master, man?"

She pointed to her husband and said, "There's thy master."

"What's the matter, Puppy?" Tobias Turf asked.

"Oh, master!" Ball Puppy said. "Oh, dame! Oh, dame! Oh, master!"

"What do thou want to say to thy master, or thy dame?" Dame Turf asked.

"Oh, John Clay! John Clay! John Clay!" Ball Puppy cried.

"What about John Clay?" Tobias Turf asked.

"May good fortune grant that he doesn't bring us news that John Clay shall be hanged!" Medley said.

"The world forfend [forbid]!" Clench said. "I hope it is not so well [he meant 'ill']."

"Oh, Lord!" John Clay said. "Oh, me, what shall I do? Poor John!"

In this society, salted fish were called "poor john."

"Oh, John Clay! John Clay! John Clay!" Ball Puppy cried.

John Clay said to himself, "Woe to me that I was ever born! I will not stay and endure it, for all the tiles in Kilburn."

Unobserved, he fled.

"What about Clay?" Dame Turf asked. "Speak, Puppy. What about him?"

Ball Puppy began, "He has lost, he has lost —"

Tobias Turf said, "For luck's sake speak, Puppy. What has he lost?"

"Oh, Audrey, Audrey, Audrey!" Ball Puppy said.

"What about my daughter, Audrey?" Dame Turf said.

Ball Puppy said, "I tell you, Audrey — do you understand me? Audrey, sweet master, Audrey, my dear dame —"

"Where is she?" Tobias Turf asked. "What's become of her, I ask thee?"

Ball Puppy said, "Oh, the serving-man! The serving-man! The serving-man!"

He was talking about Basket Hilts.

Tobias Turf asked, "Why do thou talk about the serving-man? Where's Audrey?"

"Gone with the serving-man! Gone with the serving-man!" Ball Puppy said.

"Good Puppy, where has she gone with him?" Dame Turf asked.

Ball Puppy said:

"I cannot tell.

"He bade me bring you word that the Captain was staying at the Lion, and before I came back, Audrey was gone with the serving-man.

"I tell you, Audrey's run away with the serving-man."

Tobias Turf said, "'Od 'socks, my woman, what shall we do now?"

"'Od 'socks" is a mild curse: "By God's socks."

According to the *Oxford English Dictionary*, the word "godsokers" is "Used as an exclamation or oath expressing surprise or affirmation."

Dame Turf said, "Now, if you don't help, man, I don't know, I."

Tobias Turf said, "This was your pomp — unnecessary train — of maids! I told you about it. Six maids to vollow you, and leave not one to wait upon your daughter! I zaid Pride would be paid her old vippence [fivepence] one day, wife."

In other words, pride would get its deserts.

A proverb states, "Pride goes before a fall."

A common expression of the time was "as fine as fivepence."

Dame Turf should have allowed one of her maids to wait on Audrey and serve as a chaperone.

Medley asked Ball Puppy, "What about John Clay, Ball Puppy?"

Ball Puppy began, "He has lost —"

Medley interrupted, "His life for a velony [felony]?"

Ball Puppy said, "No, his wife by villainy."

Tobias Turf said:

"Now villains both! Oh, that same hue and cry! Oh, neighbors! Oh, that cursèd serving-man! Oh, maids! Oh, wife!

"But John Clay, where is he?"

Everyone looked around for him, but he had fled.

Tobias Turf continued:

"What! Fled for vear [fear], zay ye? Will he slip us now? [Will he give us the slip now?] We who are sureties must require [inquire about and seek] 'hun [him] out.

"What shall we do to find the serving-man?

"Cock's bodikins [By God's body], we must not lose John Clay!

"Audrey, my daughter Audrey, too! Let us zend to all the towns and zeek her; but alas, the hue and cry, that must be looked to!"

If he found the serving-man, Basket Hilts, he believed that he would find his daughter, Audrey.

Squire Tub entered the scene and asked, "What, in a passion, Turf?"

Tobias Turf replied, "Aye, good Squire Tub. Honest varmers [farmers] were never thus perplexed."

Squire Tub replied:

"Turf, I am privy to — I know — thy deep unrest, the ground of which springs from an idle plot laid for a suitor to your daughter Audrey — and thus much, Turf, let me advertise [advise] you.

"I met your daughter Audrey on the way, with Justice Bramble in her company, who intends to marry her at Pancridge church. And Chanon Hugh is there ready to meet them.

"To prevent this marriage, you must not trust delay, but with wingèd speed you must cross and oppose their sly intent."

A proverb stated, "Delay in love is dangerous."

Squire Tub continued:

"So then hie — hurry — thee, Turf; hasten to forbid the bans."

He wanted Tobias Turf to stop the marriage.

Tobias Turf replied:

"Has Justice Bramble got my daughter Audrey? A little while shall he enjoy her, zure."

He meant that Justice Bramble would enjoy her for only a little while. A bawdy cynic might say that he would enjoy her for about fifteen minutes.

Tobias Turf continued:

"But oh, the hue and cry! That hinders me; I must pursue that or neglect my journey."

He could pursue the hue and cry in search of the "robbers" (and John Clay), or he would neglect his journey to take John Clay to Paddington.

Of course, if he pursued the hue and cry, he would not be able to stop the marriage of his daughter to Justice Preamble.

Tobias Turf continued:

"I'll even leave all, and with the patient ass, the over-laden ass, throw off my burden, and cast aside my office; pluck in my large ears betimes [while I have time], lest some disjudge 'em [misjudge them] to be horns."

A proverb stated, "An ass endures his burden, but not more than his burden."

In the fable "The Hare and Its Ears," a lion was angry at all animals that have horns, and so a hare avoided the lion lest the hare's long ears be mistaken for horns.

Thomas Dekker in his play *Match Me in London*, wrote, "If the lion say the ass's ears are horns, the ass, if he be wise, will swear it."

Tobias Turf continued:

"I'll leave [cease] to beat it on the broken hoof and ease my pasterns."

Tobias Turf was going to quit before he suffered any more.

Pasterns are the horse's ankles.

Tobias Turf continued:

"I'll no more High Constables."

He would no longer carry out the responsibilities of a High Constable.

Squire Tub said:

"I cannot choose but smile to see thee troubled with such a bald, half-hatchèd [badly thought-out] circumstance!

"The Captain [Chanon Hugh in disguise] was not robbed, as is reported; that trick the Justice craftily devised to break the marriage with the tile-man Clay.

"The hue and cry was merely counterfeit."

It was counterfeit because it was based on a lie.

How did Squire Tub learn this?

Earlier, Miles Metaphor had told Squire Tub that the warrant against him, supposedly from the Queen's Council, was a fake. Miles Metaphor, however, had not stated that the hue and cry against John Clay was based on a lie. Squire Tub had then left to inform Tobias Turf that Tobias' daughter was in danger of being married to Justice Preamble.

Squire Tub continued:

"The rather may you judge it to be such because the bridegroom was described to be one of the thieves, first in the velony."

The phrase "first in the velony" meant that he was the leader of the criminals committing the felony.

Squire Tub continued:

"Which, how far it is from him, yourselves may guess.

"It was Justice Bramble's vetch [fetch, aka trick], to get the wench."

Squire Tub had used his power of reasoning to figure out that the hue and cry against John Clay was based on a lie.

"And is this true, Squire Tub?" Tobias Turf asked.

Squire Tub replied, "Believe me, Turf, as I am a squire; or less, a gentleman."

A squire ranks below a knight and above a gentleman.

Some people may consider having the qualities (rather than the rank) of a gentleman to be more important than having a high social rank.

Tobias Turf said:

"I take my office back, and my authority, upon Your Worship's words."

He then said:

"Neighbors, I am High Constable again.

"Where's my zon Clay? He shall be my zon [son-in-law] yet.

"Wife, your meat by leisure: Draw back the spits."

The phrase "your meat by leisure" means "your food without haste." Tobias Turf wanted his wife to strive to keep the meat warm so it could be eaten later without being overcooked. Drawing back the spits meant that the meat would not be directly over the fire.

"That's done already, man," Dame Turf said.

Tobias Turf said:

"I'll break off this marriage between Justice Preamble and Audrey; and afterward, she shall be given to her first betrothed: John Clay.

"Look after the meat, wife, look well to the roast."

He exited with Clench, Medley, To-Pan, and Scriben.

"I'll follow him aloof — at a distance — to see the outcome," Squire Tub said.

He exited.

Ball Puppy said, "Dame, mistress, although I do not turn the spit, I hope yet to have the pig's head."

He wanted to eat the head of one of the pigs roasting on a spit.

"Come up, Jack-sauce — you impudent fellow — it shall be served to you," Dame Turf said.

"No, no service," Ball Puppy said, "but a reward for service."

"I always took you for an unmannerly Puppy," Dame Turf said. "Will you come, and vetch more wood to the vire, Master Ball?"

Ball Puppy said:

"I, vetch wood to the vire? I shall piss the vire out first. You think to make me even your ox, or ass, or anything.

"Although I cannot right myself and get revenge for myself on you, I'll sure revenge myself on your meat."

They exited.

— 3.4 —

Lady Tub, Pol-Marten, and Wisp talked together.

Pol-Marten said:

"Madam, to Kentish Town we have arrived at length, but by the way we cannot meet the Squire, nor by inquiry can we hear of him.

"Here is the house of Turf, the father of the maiden."

Lady Tub said:

"Pol-Marten, look, the streets are strewed with herbs, and here has been a wedding, Wisp, it seems! I pray to Heaven that this bridal — this wedding — is not for my son!

"Good Marten, knock; knock quickly; ask for Turf.

"My thoughts misgive me and make me apprehensive, I am in such a fear —"

Pol-Marten knocked and said loudly, "Who keeps the house here?"

From inside Tobias Turf's house, Ball Puppy answered, "Why, the door and walls keep the house."

"I ask then, who's within?" Pol-Marten asked.

"Not you who are without — outside," Ball Puppy replied.

"Look forth, and speak into the street, here," Pol-Marten said. "Come before my lady."

Ball Puppy replied:

"Before my lady! Lord have mercy upon me.

"If I come before her, she will see the handsomest man in all the town, pardee!"

"Pardee!" means "By God!"

Ball Puppy opened the door, came outside, and said, "Now stand I vore [before] her, what zaith velvet she?"

"Velvet" was a luxurious cloth. Lady Tub was wearing a velvet gown.

"Sirrah, whose man are you?" Lady Tub asked.

"Madam, my master's," Ball Puppy answered.

"And who's thy master?" Lady Tub asked.

"What you tread on, madam," Ball Puppy answered.

"I tread on an old turf," Lady Turf said.

"That Turf's my master," Ball Puppy said.

"A merry fellow!" Lady Tub said. "What's thy name?"

"They call me Ball Puppy at home; away from my home, they call me Hannibal Puppy."

Lady Tub said, "Come hither, I must kiss thee, Valentine Puppy."

She then asked, "Wisp, have you got yourself a Valentine?"

"None, madam," Wisp said. "He's the first stranger whom I saw."

According to custom, Valentines could be made by chance meetings as well as by the casting of lots.

Lady Tub said, "To me he is so, and such. Let's share him equally."

Both Lady Tub and Wisp attempted to kiss Ball Puppy.

He shouted:

"Help, help, good dame! A rescue, and in time!

"Instead of bills, come with colstaves; instead of spears, come with spits. Your slices shall serve for slicing swords, to save me and my wits. A lady and her woman here, their usher also by their side — but he stands mute — have plotted how to divide your Puppy."

Bills are weapons with long blades. Colstaves are sticks used to carry stuff; spits were used for spit-roasting. Slices are flat kitchen utensils.

Ball Puppy was calling for help from the kitchen staff, who could use common items found in kitchens as weapons.

Dame Turf and her maids came outside.

"What is this now? What noise is this with you, Ball Puppy?" Dame Turf asked.

Ball Puppy said:

"Oh, dame! And fellows of the kitchen! Arm, arm, for my safety, if you love your Ball!

"Here is a strange thing called a Lady, a mad-dame and madam, and a device of hers, yclept [called] her woman [serving-woman]."

The Lady is Lady Tub, and the device (perhaps Ball Puppy meant by "device" a puppet) is Dido Wisp.

Ball Puppy continued:

"They have plotted against me in the king's highway to steal me from myself, and cut me in halves, to make one Valentine to serve them both. This one for my right-side love, and that one for my left-hand love."

"So saucy, Puppy?" Dame Turf said. "To show no more reverence than that to my lady and her velvet gown?"

High-ranking women wore velvet gowns.

Lady Tub said:

"Turf's wife, don't rebuke him; your serving-man pleases me with his conceit. "

The conceit was the imaginative idea of splitting himself into half-Valentines.

Lady Tub then said to Ball Puppy:

"Wait, there are ten old nobles" — she gave him money — "to make thee merrier yet, half-Valentine."

"I thank you, right-side," Ball Puppy said. "If my left-side could give me as much money as you have, it would make me a man of mark: young Hannibal!"

Nobles and marks are kinds of money.

Lady Tub said:

"Dido shall make that good, or I will for her.

"Here, Dido Wisp, there's something for your Hannibal."

Lady Tub gave her money, and then she said:

"He is your countryman, as well as your Valentine."

Dido was a famous Queen of Carthage, and Hannibal was a famous general of Carthage.

Dido Wasp handed Hannibal Puppy the money and said, "Here, Master Hannibal: This is my lady's bounty for her poor woman, Wisp."

Ball Puppy said, "Brave Carthage queen! And such was Dido: I will forever be champion to her, who Juno is to thee."

The goddess Juno supported Carthage, not Rome. In an attempt to prevent the Trojan Prince Aeneas from going to Italy and becoming an important ancestor of the Romans, she made Dido fall in love with Aeneas, hoping that Aeneas would stay in Carthage.

In Ball Puppy's comparison, Lady Tub was Juno, and Dido Wisp was the Queen of Carthage.

Dame Turf said, "Your Ladyship is very welcome here. May it please you, good madam, to go near the house."

"Turf's wife, I come thus far to seek thy husband, having some business to impart to him," Ball Puppy said. "Is he at home?"

Dame Turf said:

"Oh, no, if it shall please you. He is posted hence to Pancridge, with a witness."

"With a witness" is an idiom for "hastily."

Dame Turf continued:

"Young Justice Bramble has kept level coil [made a disturbance] here in our quarters and stolen away our daughter, and Master Turf's run after, as fast as he can, to stop the marriage, if it can be stopped."

"Level coil" is the game *lever le cul*, aka changing chairs.

Pol-Marten said, "Madam, these tidings are not much amiss, for if the Justice should have the maiden in keep [under his control], you need not fear the marriage of your son to her."

Lady Tub said, "That somewhat eases my suspicious breast."

She then asked, "Tell me, Turf's wife, when was my son with Audrey? How long has it been since you saw him at your house?"

Ball Puppy said to Dame Turf, "Dame, let me take this rump out of your mouth."

Ball Puppy was pretending that he didn't want to use the word "tale," which when spelled "tail" can mean "butt," but of course the use of "rump" in this sentence is indelicate.

"What mean you by that, sir?" Dame Turf asked.

Ball Puppy said, "Rump and tail's all one. But I would use a reverence for my lady. I would not zay, sir-reverence, 'Take the tale out of your mouth,' but rather 'Take the rump.'"

"Sir-reverence," aka "save your reverence," was used to mean "excrement." It also was used to apologize for using an indelicate phrase.

"To take the tale out of someone's mouth" meant "to tell the tale for someone."

"A well-bred youth!" Dame Turf said. "And vull of favor — attractive features — you are."

Ball Puppy said:

"What might they zay, when I were gone, if I did not weigh my wordz? 'This Puppy is a vool; Great Hannibal's an ass: He had no breeding.'

"No, Lady gay [Lady Tub], you shall not zay that your Val [Valentine] Puppy was so unlucky in speech as to fail and name a tail, be as be may be, 'vore a fair lady."

"Stop jesting," Lady Tub said. "Tell us when you saw our son."

Ball Puppy began to pun on sun/son.

"By the Virgin Mary, it is two hours ago," he said.

"Since you saw him?" Lady Tub asked.

"You might have seen him too, if you had looked up," Ball Puppy said. "For it shined as bright as day."

"I mean my son," Lady Tub said.

"Your sun and our sun, are they not all one?" Ball Puppy asked.

"Fool, thou mistake my word. I asked thee for my son!" Lady Tub said.

"I had thought there had been no more suns than one," Ball Puppy said. "I know not what you ladies have — or may have."

Some ladies may have more sons than they acknowledge having.

Pol-Marten asked, "Didn't thou ever hear my lady had a son?"

Ball Puppy replied:

"She may have twenty; but for a son, unless she mean precisely Squire Tub, her zon, he was here just now, and brought my master word that Justice Bramble had got Mistress Audrey.

"But to where he has gone, here's none can tell."

Lady Tub said to Pol-Marten:

"Marten, I wonder at this strange discourse.

"The fool, it seems, is telling the truth; my son the Squire was doubtless here this morning.

"As for the match, I'll smother what I think, and staying here, I'll attend the sequel of this strange beginning."

She then said:

"Turf's wife, my people and I will trouble thee, until we hear some tidings of thy husband; the rather for my parti-Valentine."

Lady Tub and Dido Wisp would stay here at the Turfs' home partly so they could be close to their half-Valentine: Ball Puppy.

They went inside the house.

— 3.6 —

Tobias Turf, Audrey, Clench, Medley, To-Pan, and Scriben talked together.

Tobias Turf had done a heroic deed: He had rescued his daughter from a man who had attempted to carry her away and marry her. Now he was thinking about his place in future pageants celebrating heroes.

He said:

"Well, I have succeeded, and I will triumph over this justice as becomes a constable, and a High Constable."

Roman generals who won notable victories over enemy armies were allowed to ride into Rome triumphal processions with their army, spoils, and prisoners. These were great honors.

He continued:

"Next to our Saint George, who rescued the king's daughter, I will ride; I will ride ahead of Prince Arthur."

Saint George is the patron saint of England. One of his exploits was killing a dragon.

Prince Arthur may be King Arthur or, possibly, King Henry VIII's elder brother.

Tobias Turf and his friends began to discuss some other people who could appear in a pageant with the High Constable.

"Or ahead of our Shoreditch Duke," Clench said.

"Or Pancridge Earl," Medley said.

The Shoreditch Duke and the Pancridge Earl are mock-aristocratic titles given to champion archers of the Finsbury Archers.

"Or Bevis, or Sir Guy, who were both High Constables," To-Pan said.

Sir Bevis of Hampton and Sir Guy, who married the heiress of Warwick, were heroes of medieval romances.

Clench said, "One of Southampton —"

Medley said, "— the other of Warwick Castle."

Tobias Turf said, "You shall work my exploit into a story for me, neighbor Medley, over my chimney."

The story would be a narrative in pictures. Medley was a carpenter, and so the story would perhaps be an inlaid panel.

Scriben said, "I can give you, sir, a Roman story of a petty constable, who had a daughter who was called Virginia, similar to Mistress Audrey, and as young as she, and I can tell how her father bare [bore] himself in the business against Justice Appius, a decemvir in Rome, and justice of assize."

Virginia's father killed her rather than give her to the evil Appius Claudius. Livy tells the story in his *History of Rome*, Book 3, Chapters 44-49.

A decemvir was a justice, one of a group of ten, in ancient Rome.

Tobias Turf said, "That, that, good D'ogenes! A learnèd man is a chronicle."

"I can tell you a thousand stories about great Pompey, Caesar, Trajan, all the High Constables there," Scriben said.

"That was their place!" Tobias Turf said. "They were no more."

"Dictator and High Constable were both the same positions," Scriben said.

"High Constable was a higher position, though!" Medley said. "He laid Dick Tator by the heels."

"Dick Tator" is Medley's interpretation of "dictator."

"Dick Tooter!" To-Pan said.

"Dick Tooter" is To-Pan's interpretation of "Dick Tator."

To-Pan continued, "He was one of the waits — musicians — of the city, I have read about 'hun [him]. He was a fellow who would be drunk, debauched — and he did zet 'un [him] in the stocks indeed: His name was Vadian, and a cunning Tooter."

A tooter likely plays a wind instrument.

In To-Pan's dialect, V is often used for F.

A Fabian is a member of the Roman gens (family) Fabia. This was a patrician family name.

In 221 and 217 B.C.E., Quintus Fabius Maximus Verrucosis — known as Cunctator — was Roman Dictator. "Cunctator" means "Delayer," and as dictator he harassed the Carthaginian general Hannibal's army without ever fighting it in open battle. This is probably the "Vadian" To-Pan meant.

Audrey said:

"Was a silly maid ever thus posted — handed — off, who should have had three husbands in one day, yet, by bad fortune, am possessed of — the owner of, or possessed by — none?

"I went to church and would have been wed to Clay.

"Then Squire Tub seized me on the way and thought to have had me, but he missed his aim."

In bawdy terms, Squire Tub's "arrow" did not hit its feminine target.

Audrey continued:

"And Justice Bramble, nearest of the three, was almost married to me, when by chance in rushed my father and broke off that dance."

Sex can be likened to a kind of dance.

Tobias Turf said:

"Aye, girl, there's never a justice among them all who shall teach the Constable how to guard his own.

"Let's go back to Kentish Town, and there make merry. These news will be glad tidings to my wife.

"Thou shall have Clay, my wench; that word shall stand."

In Elizabethan slang the word "stand" can meant "erection."

Tobias Turf continued:

"He's found by this time, surely, or else he's drowned.

"The wedding dinner will be spoiled; make haste."

Audrey said, "Husbands, they say, grow thick but thin are sown. I don't care who my husband shall be, as long as I have one."

The word "thick" can mean "stupid."

A part of a husband can grow thick during the wedding night but then become thin once the sowing is done.

A farmer's proverb stated, "Thick sown but thin came up."

Tobias Turf said, "Aye, zay you zo? Perhaps you shall have none for that. [Perhaps you don't deserve one.]"

"Now out on me!" Audrey said. "What shall I do then?"

"Sleep, Mistress Audrey, dream about proper, handsome men," Medley said.

They exited.

— 3.7 —

Chanon Hugh and Justice Preamble talked together in Justice Preamble's house.

Chanon Hugh said:

"*O bone Deus*! [Oh, good God!] Have you seen the like?

"Here was, 'Hodge hold thine ear fair, while I strike.'"

This was an idiomatic expression for a brawl.

He continued:

"By the body of me, how did this gear — this trouble — come about?"

Justice Preamble said:

"I don't know, Chanon, but it falls out contrary to what we wanted. Nor can I make conjecture by the circumstance of these events; it was impossible, being so close and politicly — secretly and shrewdly — carried, to come so quickly to the ears of Turf.

"Oh, priest, had thy slow delivery just been nimble, and thy lazy Latin tongue you had just run the forms over with that swift dispatch — speed — as had been requisite and needed, all would have been well!"

Chanon Hugh said:

"What should have been, that never loved the friar."

A proverb stated, "What was good, the friar never loved."

In other words: It would have been good to be quick, but that's not my — Chanon Hugh's — way.

He continued:

"But thus you see the old adage verified, *multa cadunt inter* — you can guess the rest."

He then translated the Latin proverb *Multa cadunt inter calicem supremaque labra*:

"'Many things fall between the cup and lip.'"

Chanon Hugh continued:

"And though they touch, you are not sure to drink.

"You lacked good fortune, we had done our parts.

"Give a man fortune, throw him in the sea."

In other words: Good fortune is followed by bad fortune.

A play at this time was titled *Give a Man Luck and Throw Him into the Sea*. He continued:

"The properer the man, the worse the luck. Stay a time.

"*Tempus edax* — in time the stately ox, etc.

"Good counsels usually never come too late."

The Latin proverb *Tempus edax rerum* means "Time, consumer of things."

The full English proverb is "In time the savage ox does bear the yoke."

Justice Preamble said, "You, sir, will run your counsels out of breath."

Chanon Hugh said, "Spur a free horse, he'll run himself to death."

A proverb stated, "Do not spur a willing horse."

Miles Metaphor entered the scene.

Seeing him, Chanon Hugh said, "*Sancti Evangelistae*! [Oh, holy Evangelists!] Here comes Miles!"

"What is the news, man, with our new-made pursuivant?" Justice Preamble asked.

Miles Metaphor said:

"A pursuivant! I wish that I were either more pursy [like a moneybag] and had more store of money, or less pursy [fat] and had more store of breath.

"You call me pursuivant!

"But I could never vaunt of [boast about] any purse I had since you were my godfathers and godmothers and gave me that nickname."

They had given him the name of "pursuivant" and so they were his godfathers and godmothers.

"What's the matter now?" Justice Preamble asked.

"Nay, it's no matter [it's not important]," Miles Metaphor said. "I have been simply beaten."

"What has become of the Squire Tub, who was thy prisoner?" Chanon Hugh asked.

Miles Metaphor replied, "The lines of blood, which ran streaming from my head, can speak what rule the Squire has kept with me."

A ruler can be used to make lines; the Squire had used his ruling power to make lines of blood run down Metaphor's head.

"Please, Miles, relate the manner how that happened," Justice Preamble said.

Miles Metaphor replied:

"Be it known unto you by these presents then, that I, Miles Metaphor, Your Worship's clerk, have even been beaten to an allegory by a multitude of hands."

He had been beaten out of himself, aka he had been beaten so hard that he was no longer metaphor but was instead allegory — all gory.

Miles Metaphor continued:

"Had they been but some five or six, I'd whipped them all like tops in Lent, and hurled them into Hobbler's hole, or the next ditch."

Hobbler's hole is a children's game involving a top and a hole. Possibly, children would try to spin the top in such a way that it would travel to and fall in the hole.

Miles Metaphor continued:

"I would have cracked all their costards — heads — as nimbly as a squirrel will crack nuts, and flourished similar to Hercules, the porter, among the pages."

Hercules was a porter of large size who served Queen Elizabeth I.

Miles Metaphor continued:

"But when they came on like bees about a hive, crows about carrion, flies about sweetmeats, nay, like watermen [ferrymen] about a fare [a customer], then was poor Metaphor glad to give up the honor of the day and surrender, to quit his charge to them, and run away to save his life, only to tell this news."

Chanon Hugh said:

"How indirectly — how contrary — all things have fallen out!

"I cannot choose but wonder who they were who rescued your rival from the keep of Miles Metaphor.

"But most of all, I cannot well digest in what way Tobias Turf came to learn our plot."

Justice Preamble said:

"Miles, I will see that all thy wounds are medically dressed.

"As for the Squire Tub's escape, it doesn't matter. We have by this means disappointed him, and that was all the main thing I aimed at.

"But Chanon Hugh, now muster up thy wits, and call thy thoughts into the consistory — the ecclesiastical court. Search all the secret corners of thy priest's four-cornered cap to find another ingenious scheme to disappoint and stop her marriage with this Clay.

"Do that, and I'll reward thee jovially."

"Jovially" means "in the manner of the god Jupiter" — that is, handsomely.

Chanon Hugh replied, "Well said, Magister [Scholar] Justice. If I don't fit you with such a new and well-laid stratagem as never yet your ears did hear a finer, call me with Lily *Bos, Fur, Sus, atque Sacerdos.*"

The Latin words, which mean "bull/cow, thief, boar/sow, and priest/priestess," come from W. Lily's *Brevissima institutio seu ratio grammatices* (1567), a Latin grammar.

In other words: If I don't come up with a new good plan, class me among the animals.

Justice Preamble said, "I hear there's comfort in thy words yet, Chanon. I'll trust thy regulars and say no more."

The Latin word *regula* means "grammatical rule."

Chanon Hugh was part of the regular clergy.

Justice Preamble and Chanon Hugh exited.

Miles Metaphor said to himself, "I'll follow, too. And if the dapper priest be just as cunning, point in his device [skillful in his plot], as I was in my lie, my master Preamble will stalk as if led by the nose with these new promises and fatted with supposes — expectations — of fine hopes."

Miles Metaphor's lie was that Squire Tub had been freed by men who had fought Miles. Instead, Basket Hilts had intimidated him, and Miles Metaphor had quickly released Squire Tub and told him about the plot by Justice Preamble and Chanon Hugh. Squire Tub had then informed Tobias Turf.

— 3.8 —

Tobias Turf, Dame Turf, Lady Tub, Pol-Marten, Audrey, and Ball Puppy spoke together at the Turfs' house.

"Well, madam, I may thank the Squire, your son," Tobias Turf said to Lady Tub. "If not for him, I would have been outwitted."

Squire Tub had let the High Constable know that Justice Preamble had Audrey.

"May Heaven's blessing alight upon his heart now!" Dame Turf said. "We are beholden to him, indeed, madam."

"But can you inform me where he is?" Lady Tub asked. "And can you inform me about what he intended?"

"Madam, whatever he intended was no whit concerning me, and therefore was I less inquisitive," Tobias Turf said. "Whatever he intended had nothing to do with me."

Of course, he was wrong. Squire Tub had intended to marry Audrey. This is something that Squire Tub did not tell Tobias Turf.

Lady Tub said to Audrey, "Fair maiden, in faith, speak truth and do not dissemble. Doesn't he often come and visit you?"

Audrey answered, "His Worship now and then, if it please you, takes pains to see my father and mother; but as for me, I know that I am too mean — of too lowly birth — for his high thoughts to stoop at, more than asking a light question to make him merry, or to pass his time."

Lady Tub said, "You are a sober and serious maiden."

She then ordered, "Call for my serving-woman, Marten."

Her serving-woman was Dido Wisp.

Pol-Marten said, "The maids and her half-Valentine have plied her with courtesy of the bride-cake and the bowl, and so she is tipsy and lying down for a while."

Lady Tub said:

"Oh, let her rest! We will cross over to Canonbury in the interim, and so make for home.

"Farewell, good Turf, and thy wife. I wish your daughter joy."

Tobias Turf said, "We give thanks to Your Ladyship."

Lady Tub and Pol-Marten exited.

Tobias Turf asked his wife, "Where is John Clay now? Have you seen him yet?"

Dame Turf said, "No, he has hidden himself out of the way because of fear of the hue and cry."

Tobias Turf said:

"What, does that shadow walk avore 'un [before him] still?"

In 3.3 Squire Tub had told him that the hue and cry in search of John Clay was a counterfeit: It was based on a lie.

Tobias Turf continued:

"Puppy, go seek 'un [him] out. Search all the corners that he frequents, and call 'un [him] forth.

"We'll go once more to the church and try our vortunes.

"Luck, son Valentine!

"Where are all the wise men of Finzbury?"

Ball Puppy replied:

"Where wise men should be: at the ale and bride-cake.

"I wish that this couple had their destiny — either to be hanged or to be married — out of the way. A man cannot get the mountenance [amount] of an eggshell to stay his stomach."

Some neighbors arrived on the scene and walked over to Tobias Turf.

Ball Puppy continued:

"Vaith, vor my own part, I have zupped up so much broth as would have covered a leg of beef over head and ears [that is, completely immersed it] in the porridge-pot, and yet I cannot sussify [satisfy] wild nature.

"I wish that they were at once dispatched [married] so that we might go to dinner.

"I am with child of a huge stomach, and long for food, until by some honest midwife-piece-of-beef I am delivered of it."

He was hungry with urgings for food like a pregnant woman, but the marriage had not occurred and so he could not eat yet. A piece of beef would satisfy his huge appetite and stop his hunger pangs the way a midwife stops birth pains.

Ball Puppy concluded:

"I must go now and hunt out for this Kilburn calf, John Clay, whom I don't know where to find, nor which way to go."

A "calf" is a fool.

Ball Puppy exited.

Chanon Hugh, in the personage of Captain Thumbs, entered the scene.

He said to you, the readers:

"Thus as a beggar in a king's disguise, or an old cross well sided with [standing beside] a maypole, comes Chanon Hugh, accoutered as you see, disguised soldado-like. Note his scheme."

A soldado is a soldier.

He continued:

"The Chanon is that Captain Thumbs, who was robbed.

"These bloody scars created with makeup upon my face are wounds. This scarf upon my arm shows my recent wounds, And thus am I to gull — fool — the constable.

"Now you have a man at arms among you! Look out! I'm a soldier!"

He then asked out loud:

"Friends, by your leave, which of you is the man named Turf?"

Tobias Turf answered, "Sir, I am Turf, if you want to speak with me."

"Yes, with thee, Turf, if thou are High Constable," the disguised Chanon Hugh said.

"I am both Turf, sir, and High Constable," Tobias Turf said.

The disguised Chanon Hugh said:

"Then, Turf or Scurf, high or low constable, know that I was once a captain at the Battle of Saint Quentins in northern France, and passing across the ways over the country this morning, between this place — Kentish Town — and Hampstead Heath, I was by a crew of clowns robbed, bobbed [buffeted], and hurt."

"Scurf" is flakes of skin. An example: dandruff. The word can also mean a scab.

The disguised Chanon Hugh continued:

"No sooner had I got my wounds bound up, but with much pain I went to the next justice, one Master Bramble, here at Maribone, and here a warrant is, which he has directed for you, one Turf — if your name is Toby Turf — who have let fall and allowed to lapse, they say, the hue and cry.

"And you shall answer it before the Justice."

He presented a warrant to Tobias Turf.

"Heaven and Hell, dogs, devils, what is this!" Tobias Turf said. "Neighbors, was ever any constable thus crossed? What shall we do?"

In 3.3 Squire Tub had told Tobias Turf that the hue and cry in search of John Clay was a counterfeit: It was based on a lie. Tobias Turf, however, still believed that a man named Captain Thumbs had been attacked, although not by John Clay.

"Truly, we all must go hang ourselves," Medley said. "I know no other way to escape the law."

Ball Puppy entered the scene and said, "News, news! Oh, news —"

"What, have thou found out where John Clay is?" Tobias Turf asked.

"No, sir, the news is that I cannot find him," Ball Puppy said.

The disguised Chanon Hugh asked Tobias Turf:

"Why do you dally, you damned russet coat?"

Peasants wore russet coats.

He continued:

"You peasant, you clown, you constable!

"See that you bring forth the suspected party, or by my honor — which I won on the battlefield — I'll make you pay for it before the Justice."

Tobias Turf said:

"Darn! Darn!

"Oh, wife, I'm now in a fine pickle.

"He who was most suspected is not found, and what now makes me think that he did the deed is that he thus absents him and dares not be seen."

Now Tobias Turf was again thinking that John Clay was guilty of robbery.

He continued:

"Captain, my innocence will plead for me.

"Wife, I must go, necessarily and reluctantly, for I am the one whom the devil drives. Pray for me, wife and daughter, pray for me."

The disguised Chanon Hugh said, "I'll lead the way."

He then said to himself, "Thus is the wedding-match put off, and if my plot succeeds, as I have laid it, my captainship shall cost him in fines many a crown."

The disguised Chanon Hugh, Tobias Turf, and the neighbors exited.

Dame Turf said sarcastically, "So, we have brought our eggs to a fair market."

She then said, "Curse that villain Clay! Would he do a robbery? I'll never trust any smooth-faced tile-man for his sake."

Audrey said, "Mother, the still sow eats up all the draff [pig swill]."

In other words: The quiet ones get it all.

Audrey and Dame Turf exited.

Alone, Ball Puppy said:

"Thus is my master, Toby Turf, the pattern of all the painful adventures now in print!"

Lawrence Twine had written a prose romance titled *The Pattern of Painful Adventures* (1576).

Ball Puppy continued:

"I never could hope better of this match, this bride-ale, because of what happened the night before today — which is within man's memory, I take it —"

Ball Puppy now listed many bad omens — the wedding feast was ominous for all the farm animals that were slain to provide the food for the feast.

The first omen — the talking ox — has a precedent in literature. In Livy's *History of Rome*, Book 35, Chapter 21, Line 4, he wrote about an ox speaking and advising the Romans to beware before the Roman war with Antiochus (192 B.C.E.).

Ball Puppy continued:

"— at the first report of the wedding, an ox did speak, who died soon after; a cow lost her calf; the bell-wether sheep was flayed — skinned — for it; a fat hog was singed, and washed, and shaven all over, to remove its bristles so it would look ugly in preparation for this day; the ducks they quacked; the hens also cackled, at the noise whereof a drake was seen to dance a headless round; the goose was cut in the head to hear it, too."

Fowl such as chickens will flap their wings soon after their heads are cut off with an axe.

Ball Puppy continued:

"Brave Chant-it-clear, his noble heart was done, his comb was cut, and two or three of his wives, or fairest concubines, had their necks broken before they would zee this day."

Chanticleer is a traditional name for a cock.

Ball Puppy continued:

"To mark the verven' [fervent] heart of a beast, the very pig, the pig this very morning, as he was a-roasting, cried out his eyes, and made a show as if he would have bit in two the spit, as if he would say, 'There shall no roast meat be this dismal day.'"

Grease dripping from the eyes is a sign that the pig is fully roasted or close to it.

Ball Puppy continued:

"And zure [surely], I think, if I had not gotten his tongue between my teeth and eaten it, he would have spoken it.

"Well, I will go in and cry, too; I will never stop crying until our maids may drive a buck — soak the clothes — with my salt tears at the next washing day."

According to the *Oxford English Dictionary*, the phrase "to drive the buck" means "to carry through the process of bucking." "Buck-washing" is a form of bleaching in which clothing is soaked or boiled in alkaline lye as the first part of the process.

He exited.

CHAPTER 4

— 4.1 —

Justice Preamble, Chanon Hugh (disguised as Captain Thumbs), Tobias Turf, and Miles Metaphor talked together in Justice Preamble's house in Maribone.

Justice Preamble said:

"Keep out those fellows; I'll have none come in but the High Constable, the man of peace, and the queen's Captain, the brave man of war.

"Now, neighbor Turf, the reason why you are called before me by my warrant, but unspecified and not yet made clear in the warrant, is this, and please note it thoroughly!

"Here is a gentleman, Captain Thumbs, and, as it seems, both of good birth, fair speech, and peaceable, who was this morning robbed here in the wood.

"You, for your part, a man of good report and reputation, of credit, landed [owner of land] and of fair demesnes [domains], and by authority High Constable, are notwithstanding touched in this complaint, of being careless and not acting diligently in the hue and cry.

"I cannot choose but grieve a soldier's loss, and I am sorry, too, for your neglect of your duty, since you are my neighbor. This is all I accuse you of."

The disguised Chanon Hugh said:

"This is not all; I can allege far more, and almost argue that he is an accessary to the robbery.

"Good Master Justice, give me permission to speak, for I am the plaintiff. Don't let his living in the neighborhood make him secure, and don't let him stand on his privilege as High Constable."

Justice Preamble said, "Sir, I dare use no partiality. Accuse him then of what you please, as long as it is the truth."

This sentence is ambiguous: It can mean 1) Accuse him then of what you please, as long as you truthfully accuse him, or 2) Accuse him then of what you please, as long as what you accuse him of is him being truthful.

The disguised Chanon Hugh said, "This more — and which is more than he can answer — beside his letting fall the hue and cry, he protects the man charged with the felony, and keeps him hidden, I hear, within his house, because he is affianced and engaged to his daughter."

Tobias Turf said:

"I do defy 'hun [repudiate him]; so shall she do, too.

"I ask Your Worship's favor, let me have hearing.

"I do convess, I was told of such a velony, and it disgrieved me not a little, when it was told to me, vor I was going to church to give Audrey away in marriage; and who should marry her but this very Clay, who was charged to be the chief thief o'hun [of them] all.

"Now I — may the halter stick me [may I be hanged] if I tell your worships any leazins [lies] — did forethink 'un [previously think that he] was the truest man, until he waz run away.

"I thought I had had 'un [him] as zure as in a zawpit, or in my oven, or in the town pound [lock-up]."

A sawpit is a hole in the ground.

He continued:

"I was zo zure o'hun [of him], I'd have given my life for 'un [him], until he did escape and run away.

"But now I zee 'un guilty, az var as I can look at 'un [as far as I can see]. Would you have more?"

Tobias Turf was again thinking that John Clay was guilty of robbery.

The disguised Chanon Hugh said:

"Yes, I will have, sir, what the law will give me.

"You gave your word to see him safe forthcoming; I challenge that [I call on you to make it good], but that is forfeited.

"Besides, your carelessness in the pursuit is evidence of your slackness and neglect of duty, which ought to be punished with severity."

Justice Preamble said:

"He speaks but reason, Turf. Bring forth the man, and you are quit; but otherwise, your word binds you to make amends for all his loss. And think yourself befriended and let off lightly, if he takes it without a farther suit or going to law.

"Come to an agreement with him, Turf. The law is costly, and it will draw on charge — it will be expensive."

Tobias Turf said:

"Yes, I do know, I vurst mun vee a returney [I first must fee an attorney], and then make legs — bow down to and request — my great man of law to be of my counsel and take trouble-vees [trouble-fees = money from me], and yet zay nothing vor me, but devise all district [strict, harsh] means to ransackle [ransack] me of my money."

Some lawyers take fees, but then they do nothing for the money.

Tobias Turf continued:

"May a pestilence prick the throats of hun [him]! I do know hun [him], as well az if I waz in their bellies, and brought up there.

"What would you have me do? What would you ask of me?"

The disguised Chanon Hugh said:

"I ask the restitution of my money taken from me in the theft, and I will not abate one penny of the sum: fourscore and five pounds. I ask in addition for amendment for my hurts; my pain and suffering are loss enough for me, sir, to sit down with — that is, to put up with.

"I'll put it to Your Worship; what you award me I'll take, and I will give him a general release."

Justice Preamble asked, "And what do you say now, neighbor Turf?"

Tobias Turf said:

"I put it rather to Your Worship's bitterment [arbitrement, aka arbitration], hab, nab."

"Hab, nab" means "however it may turn out, win or lose."

Tobias Turf continued:

"I shall have a chance of the dice for it, I hope, let them even run, and —"

He meant that he hoped that he would win. A win in this situation would be a small fine.

Justice Preamble said to the disguised Chanon Hugh, "Faith, then I'll pray you, because he is my neighbor, to take a hundred pounds and to give him day — to let him off."

The hundred pounds were for the fourscore and five pounds the disguised Chanon Hugh said that he — Captain Thumbs — had been robbed of, plus fifteen pounds for pain and suffering.

Of course, no robbery and no pain and suffering had occurred. Justice Preamble and Chanon Hugh were defrauding Tobias Turf. A judge and a clergyman were committing a crime against the High Constable.

"Saint Valentine's Day, I will, this very day, before sunset," the disguised Chanon Hugh said. "My bond is forfeit otherwise."

The bond was the warrant to have Tobias Turf arrested.

"Where will you have it paid?" Tobias Turf asked.

The disguised Chanon Hugh said, "In faith, I am a stranger here in the country. Do you know Chanon Hugh, the vicar of Pancras?"

"Yes, who doesn't know him?" Tobias Turf said.

"I'll make him my attorney to receive it, and I'll give you a discharge of the charges against you," the disguised Chanon Hugh said.

"Whom shall I send for the money?" Tobias Turf asked.

"Why, if you please, send Metaphor, my clerk," Justice Preamble said. "And, Turf, I much commend thy willingness. It's evidence of thy integrity."

Tobias Turf said:

"But my integrity shall be myzelf still.

"Good Master Metaphor, give my wife this key, and do but whisper it — give it secretly — into her hand. She knows it well enough.

"Bid her, by that, to deliver to you the two zealed bags of silver that lie in the corner of the cupboard that stands at my bedside — they're vifty pounds apiece — and bring them to your master."

Miles Metaphor said:

"If I don't prove to be as good a carrier as my friend Tom Long was, then call me his curtal, and change my name of Miles to Guiles, Wiles, Piles, Biles, or the foulest name you can devise, to play the game of crambo with for ale."

Tom Long was proverbially a dilatory carrier.

A curtal is a horse or a dog with a docked tail.

The word "guiles" means "deceit" and "insidious intelligence." The word "wiles" means "deceitful tricks." The word "piles" means "hemorrhoids." Bile is a secretion of the liver, and it is anger. The foulest name may be the vilest name, and so Viles'.

Crambo is a game in which a word is given and players have to find a rhyme for it.

The disguised Chanon Hugh said quietly to Miles Metaphor:

"Come here, Miles.

"Bring by that token, too, fair Audrey. Say that her father has sent for her. Say that John Clay has been found and waits at Pancras church, where I am waiting to marry them in haste.

"For by this means, Miles, I may say it to thee, thy master must be married to Audrey.

"But say not a word but instead be mum! Go, get thee gone. Be wary of thy charge and keep it close and secret."

Miles Metaphor said quietly, "O super-dainty Chanon! Vicar incony! [Fine vicar!] Make no delay, Miles, but go away, and bring the wench and money."

He exited.

The disguised Chanon Hugh said to Tobias Turf:

"Now, sir, I see you meant but honestly and except that business calls me hence away, I would not leave you until the sun were lower —"

He whispered to Justice Preamble:

"But Master Justice, one word, sir, with you.

"By the same token is your mistress sent for by Metaphor, your clerk, as from her father, who, when she comes, I'll marry her to you, unwitting [unknown] to this Tobias Turf, who shall wait for me at the parsonage."

He said to himself:

"This was my plot, which I must now make good; I must turn back into Chanon Hugh again, in my square cap."

The disguised Chanon Hugh then said out loud:

"I humbly take my leave."

Justice Preamble said:

"Adieu, good Captain Thumbs."

The disguised Chanon Hugh exited.

Justice Preamble then said:

"Trust me, neighbor Turf, he seems to be a sober gentleman, but this distress has somewhat stirred his patience, and men, you know, in such extremities don't incline themselves to points of courtesy.

"I'm glad you have made this end."

Tobias Turf said:

"You stood as my friend, and I thank Your Justice-Worship.

"I ask me to be prezent soon at the tendering of the money, and zee me have a discharge, vor I have no craft in your law quiblins."

"Craft" is "trickery."
"Quiblins" are quibbles and tricks.
Justice Preamble said, "I'll secure you, neighbor."
They exited.

— The Scene Interloping —
[An Unauthorized and Unlicensed Scene]

Medley, Clench, To-Pan, and Scriben talked together.

Medley said:

"Indeed there is a woundy [very great] luck in names, sirs, and a main mystery, if a man knew where to vind it.

"My godsire's name, I'll tell you, was In-and-In Shittle, and a weaver he was, and it did fit his craft, for so his shittle went in and in still, this way, and then that way.

"And he named me In-and-In Medley; this name serves a joiner's craft, because we do lay things in and in, in our work. But I am truly *architectonicus professor*, rather, that is, as one would zay, an architect."

"Shittle" is a mispronunciation of "shuttle."

Joiners sometimes do inlay work.

An *architectonicus professor* is a professor of architecture.

Clench said, "As I am a varrier and a visicary [a farrier and a physician/ apothecary], horse-smith of Hampstead, and the whole town leech [doctor] —"

Clench medically treats people as well as horses.

Medley interrupted, "Yes, you have done woundy [very great] cures, gossip [friend] Clench."

Clench said:

"If I can zee the stale [urine] once through a urine-hole, I'll give a shrewd guess, be it man or beast."

One hopes that "urine-hole" is a mispronunciation of "urinal."

The shrewd guess would be about the illness and its cure.

Clench continued:

"I cured an ale-wife once who had the staggers worse than five horses, without rowelling."

An ale-wife with the staggers may be a drunk ale-wife.

"Staggers" is also a horse disease.

"Rowelling" was a medical treatment for horses. It involved placing a piece of leather with a hole in it between the skin and flesh.

Clench continued:

"My godphere [godfather] was a Rabian [an Arabian] or a Jew — you can tell, D'oge, about 'un [him] — they called 'un [him] Doctor Rasi."

"One Rasis was a great Arabic doctor," Scriben said.

"He was King Harry's doctor, and my godphere [godfather]," Clench said.

Doctor Rasi was King Henry VIII's physician.

A famous Arabian physician was known as Rhazes (Mohammed-ben-Zakaria).

To-Pan said, "My godphere [godfather] was a merry-Greek [merry companion], To-Pan of Twyford, a jovial tinker, and a stopper of holes, who left me metal-man of Belsize, his heir."

"A stopper of holes" has a bawdy meaning.

"But who was godphere [godfather], D'oge?" Medley asked.

D'ogenes Scriben said:

"Vaith, I cannot tell if mine were kursined [christened] or not, but I am zure he had a kursin [Christian] name that he left me, Diogenes.

"A mighty learned man, but pestilence-poor — that is, extremely, plaguy poor — vor he had no house, save an old tub, to dwell in — I vind that in records — and always he turned the tub in the wind's teeth, so it blew on his backside, and there they would lie routing — roaring — one at the other a week, sometimes."

Diogenes was an ancient Greek philosopher who rejected wealth and lived in a tub or barrel. According to D'ogenes Scriben, he farted into the wind.

That's not a good idea. Neither is spitting into the wind.

"Thence came a tale of a tub," Medley said, "and the virst tale of a tub, old D'ogenes' tub."

"That was avore [before] Sir Peter Tub or his lady," Scriben said.

"Aye, or the Squire their son, Tripoly Tub," To-Pan said.

"The Squire is a fine gentleman!" Clench said.

"He is more: a gentleman and a half, almost a knight — within zix inches. That's his true measure," Medley said.

"Zure, you can gauge — measure — 'hun [him]," Clench said.

Medley said:

"To a streak, aka mark, or less; I know his diameters and circumference."

According to the *Oxford English Dictionary*, a circumference is "That which surrounds, environment."

According to the *Oxford English Dictionary*, a diameter is "the diametrical or direct opposite; contrarity, contradiction."

The direct opposite of "that which surrounds" is that which is surrounded: If it isn't surrounding, it is surrounded. In this context, that would be an interior life: thoughts and emotions. The environment is part of the exterior life: the place where one lives and acts.

Medley is claiming to know the Squire inside and out.

Medley continued:

"A knight is six diameters, and a squire is vive [five] and zomewhat more; I know it by the compass and scale of man."

According to the *Oxford English Dictionary*, "compass" means "Artifice, skilful or crafty device."

People's guilt or innocence can be weighed in the scales of justice.

Knights are supposed to be gentlemen, and any knight who uses immoral and crafty devices and plots will be found guilty when weighed in the scales of justice. This kind of character is diametrically opposite to the character a knight should have.

Knights are supposed to abide by a higher standard of chivalry than squires and so they have more dimensions, aka diameters. More is expected of knights than is expected of squires. Knights are supposed to encompass a greater portion and quality of nobility.

Medley continued: "I have upon my rule here the just perportions [proportions] of a knight, a squire; with a tame justice, or an officer rampant [upright] upon the bench, from the High Constable down to the headborough, or tithingman, or meanest — lowest in rank — minister of the peace, God save 'un [him]."

"Rampant" means "upright"; a lion rampant is a lion standing on its hind legs.

To-Pan said, "Why, you can tell us by the squire, neighbor, whence he is called a constable, and whaffore [wherefore]."

"Squire" can mean 1) esquire, and/or 2) a mason's square.

"No, that's a book-case," Medley said. "Scriben can do that. That's writing and reading, and records."

"Book-case" means "something that needs to be explained in words, not with math."

Scriben said, "Two words, *cyning* and *staple*, make a constable, or as we'd say, a hold or stay for the king."

"Cyning" is an old spelling for "king."

"Staple" means "supporting thing," such as a column that supports a roof.

"All constables are truly Johns-for-the-king, whatever their names are, be they Tony or Roger," Clench said.

"John" is a name associated with servants. A song of the time was titled "John for the King."

"And all are sworn, as vingars [fingers] on one hand, to hold together against the breach of the peace," Medley said. "The High Constable is the thumb, as one would zay, the holdfast of the rest."

A "holdfast" is something that binds.

To-Pan said, "Let's hope to luck that he speed well in the business between Captain Thumbs and him!"

Medley said:

"I'll warrant 'un [him] for a groat — I'll put my money on him.

"I have his measures here in arithmetic [written down in figures], how he should bear 'unself [himself] in all the lines of his place and office.

"Let's zeek 'un [him] out."

They exited.

Squire Tub and Basket Hilts talked together.

"Hilts, how do thou like this, our good day's work?" Squire Tub asked.

"As good even never a whit, as never the better," Basket Hilts replied.

In other words: A waste of time.

"Shall we go to Pancridge or shall we go to Kentish Town, Hilts?" Squire Tub asked.

"Let Kentish Town or Pancridge come to us, if either will," Basket Hilts said. "I will go home again."

Squire Tub said:

"Indeed, Basket, our success has been but bad, and nothing prospers that we undertake, for we can neither meet with John Clay, nor Audrey, nor the Chanon Hugh, nor Tobias Turf the constable.

"We are like men who wander in strange woods and lose ourselves in search of those whom we seek."

Basket Hilts said:

"This was because we rose on the wrong side of the bed.

"But as I am now here, just in the midway, I'll zet my sword on the pommel, and that line the point valls [falls] to we'll take, whether it be to Kentish Town, the church, or home again."

The pommel is the rounded knob at the end of a sword's hilt. To make a decision about which way to go, a person would set a sword on its pommel and let it go. Whichever way the sword pointed when it fell, that way the person would go.

Miles Metaphor, who was still disguised as the pursuivant, entered the scene, but he did not see Squire Tub or Basket Hilts. Miles Metaphor was walking to the Turfs' house at Kentish Town.

Seeing him, Squire Tub said, "Stop, stop thy hand. Here's Justice Bramble's clerk. The unlucky hare has crossed us all this day. I'll stand aside while thou pump out of him his business, Hilts, and how he's now employed."

When an unlucky cat — a black cat — crosses the way ahead of one, it's supposed to be bad luck in this culture. Miles Metaphor was an unlucky hare:

Hares are thought to be timid; after all, they are prey, not predators. Miles Metaphor was timid.

"Leave it to me," Basket Hilts said. "I'll treat him as he deserves."

Miles Metaphor said to himself:

"Oh, for a pad-horse [an easily padding — easy-paced — horse], pack-horse, or a post-horse, to bear me on his neck, his back, or his croup [hind quarters]!

"I am as weary with running as a mill-horse that has led the mill once, twice, thrice about, after the breath has been out of his body.

"I could get up upon a pannier, a panel, or, to say the truth, a very pack-saddle, until all my honey were turned into gall, and I could sit in the seat no longer."

A pannier is a basket for carrying goods, and a panel is a saddle-cloth: a cloth placed under the saddle.

Miles Metaphor was tired of walking, and he would like to ride a horse until he became tired of riding.

He continued:

"Oh, for the legs of a lackey now, or a footman, who is the surbater of a clerk courant [running clerk], and the confounder of his trestles dormant [sleeping tables]!"

Lackeys are servants who do a lot of running around as they serve their master, and footmen run beside the coach of their master. Actually, lackeys are footmen, and they are especially running footmen.

A surbater is a person who makes another person footsore. Here it may mean "outrunner." They outrun the clerk courant, whose feet become sore as he tries to catch up.

"To surbate" means "to make footsore."

A trestle table is a table made of one or more boards laid on top of trestles; trestles are frameworks that have a beam that is supported by two pairs of sloping legs.

The trestles dormant [sleeping tables] are the tables the clerks rest their heads on and sleep instead of working.

Miles Metaphor wants to have the legs of a footman so his feet will be accustomed to all the walking he is doing and so won't be sore.

Basket Hilts came forward.

Seeing him, Miles Metaphor said, "But who have we here, just in the nick?"

"Nick" means 1) at the critical moment, 2) in a tight place, or 3) the devil.

"I am neither Nick, nor in the nick," Basket Hilts said. "Therefore you lie, Sir Metaphor."

These were fighting words: "You lie."

"Lie!" Miles Metaphor said. "How?"

"Lie so, sir," Basket Hilts said.

He knocked him down.

"I lie not yet in my throat," Miles Metaphor said.

Being accused of lying in one's throat was the worst kind of accusation of lying.

"Thou lie on the ground," Basket Hilts said. "Do thou know me?"

"Yes, I did know you too late," Miles Metaphor said.

If he had seen him earlier, he could have avoided meeting him.

"What is my name, then?" Basket Hilts asked.

"Basket," Miles Metaphor answered.

"Basket what?" Basket Hilts asked.

Miles Metaphor said, "Basket the great —"

"The great what?" Basket Hilts asked.

Miles Metaphor said, "Lubber — I should say, lover of the Squire, his master."

A "lubber" is a lout.

Basket Hilts said:

"Great is my patience to forbear thee thus, thou scrapehill scoundrel, and thou scum of man! Uncivil, orange-tawny-coated clerk!"

A scrapehill is a person who rakes dunghills.

Basket Hilts continued:

"Thou came but half a thing into the world, and were made up of patches, parings, shreds.

"Thou, who when last thou were put out of service, travelled to Hampstead Heath on an Ash Wednesday, where thou did stand six weeks the Jack of Lent for boys to hurl things, three throws a penny, at thee, to make thee some money to put in a purse."

A Jack of Lent is a stuffed puppet that serves as a target for boys to throw things at.

A purse is a bag for money.

Basket Hilts continued:

"Do thou see this bold, bright blade? This sword shall shred thee as small unto the grave as minced meat for a pie.

"I'll set all of thee in earth, except thy head and thy right arm, which shall be at liberty to keep thy hat off to show respect to me, while I question thee what, why, and whither thou were going now, with a face ready to break out — erupt — with business.

"And tell me truly, lest I dash it in pieces."

Miles Metaphor said, "Then, Basket, put thy smiter — thy sword — up and hear what I say. I don't dare tell the truth to a drawn sword."

Hilts sheathed his sword and said, "It is sheathed; stand up and speak without fear or wit [cunning]."

Miles Metaphor stood up and said:

"I don't know what they mean; but Constable Turf sends here his key for monies in his cupboard, which he must pay the Captain who was robbed this morning.

"Do you smell anything?"

He meant: Do you smell a trick?

Basket Hilts said, "No, not I. Thy breeches yet are honest."

He meant that they were not yet soiled.

Miles Metaphor said:

"As is my mouth.

"Don't you smell a rat?

"I tell you the truth: I think all's knavery. For the Chanon whispered to me in my ear, when Turf had given me his key, to by the same token bring Mistress Audrey as if her father has sent for her to come thither, and to say that John Clay has been found — which is indeed to get the wench forth for my master, who is to be married when she comes there. The Chanon has his rules — his prayer book — ready and all there to dispatch the matter."

Squire Tub came forward and said:

"Now, on my life, this is the Chanon's plot!

"Miles, I have heard all thy discourse to Basket. Will thou be true and loyal to me? I'll reward thee well, if thou make me happy in my Mistress Audrey."

Miles Metaphor said, "Your Worship shall dispose of Metaphor through all his parts, even from the sole of the head to the crown of the foot, to be fully in your service."

Squire Tub said:

"Then give thy message to the Mistress Turf:

"Tell her thy token, bring the money here, and likewise take young Audrey into thy charge.

"That done, then here, Metaphor, we will wait, and intercept and meet thee. And for thy reward, you two — you and Basket Hilts — shall share the money, and I will have the maiden.

"If anyone should take offence, I'll make all good."

Miles Metaphor asked, "But shall I have half the money, sir, indeed?"

"Aye, on my squireship and my land, I swear thou shall," Squire Tub said.

Miles Metaphor said:

"Then if I don't make, sir, the cleanliest excuse to get her hither, and be then as careful to keep her for you as if it were for myself, then get down on your knees, and pray that honest Miles may break his neck before he get over two stiles."

Squire Tub replied, "Make haste, then; we will wait here for thy return."

Miles Metaphor exited, and Squire Tub said:

"This unlooked-for luck has revived my hopes, which were oppressed with a dark melancholy.

"In happy time we lingered on the way to meet these summons of a better sound, which are the essence of my soul's content."

Basket Hilts said:

"This heartless — cowardly — fellow, shame to serving-men, stain of all liveries, disgrace to his uniform, what fear makes him do!

"What sordid, ignoble, wretched, and unworthy things he does!

"Betray his master's secrets, open the closet of his master's plots, force the foolish Justice to make way for your love, plotting of his own —

"He is like a man who digs a trap to catch another man but falls into it himself!"

Squire Tub said, "So would I have it, and I hope it will prove a jest to twit — mock — the Justice with."

"But that this poor white-livered, cowardly rogue should do it!" Basket Hilts said. "And only out of fear!"

"And hope of money, Hilts," Squire Tub said. "Even a valiant man will nibble at that bait."

"Who but a fool will refuse money offered to him?" Basket Hilts, who was hoping to get fifty pounds soon, said.

"And sent by so good chance and fortune?" Squire Tub said. "Pray heaven he speed and succeed."

Basket Hilts said, "If he comes back empty-handed, let him count on going back empty-headed; I'll not leave him so much of brain in his pate, with pepper and vinegar, that could be served in for sauce to a calf's head."

In the slang of the time, a calf is a fool.

"Thou treat him rightly, Hilts," Squire Tub said.

Basket Hilts said:

"I'll seal az much with my hand as I dare say now with my tongue."

He shook hands with Squire Tub and asked:

'But if you get the lass [away?] from Dargison, what will you do with her?"
The lass is Audrey.

"Dargison" may mean "son of darg." In Scottish dialect, "darg" is a day's work. Squire Tub may be calling Justice Preamble a working man as an insult. Basket Hilts had just referred to "the foolish Justice" and Squire Tub was hoping to twit Justice Preamble. Certainly, many people were working hard on this day to marry Audrey or to get Audrey married.

But perhaps "Dargison" is Miles Metaphor, Justice Preamble's clerk, who was getting Audrey and bringing her to Squire Tub. Now Miles was working for Squire Tub and so he was a working man.

"Dargasson" means "de lad" or "de boy." The French *le gamin* means "the boy" or "the lad," and the French *gosse* means "lad, kid, brat." This could be Miles Metaphor.

Squire Tub said, "We'll think of that when once we have her in possession, governor."

Ball Puppy, Miles Metaphor, and Audrey talked together in the Turfs' house.

Ball Puppy said:

"You see we trust you, Master Metaphor, with Mistress Audrey. Please, treat her well, as a gentlewoman should be treated.

"For my part, I do incline a little and am sympathetic to the serving-man. We have been of a coat — that is, we were in the same occupation. I had a coat like yours, until it did play me such a sleeveless — pointless — errand as I had nothing where [nowhere] to put my arms in, and then I threw it off."

Sleeves have ends.

"Err ends" might be nonexistent sleeves.

And nonexistent ends might be "air ends."

Ball Puppy continued:

"Please, go before her and walk in front of her, like a serving-man, and see that your nose does not run and drop.

"For an example, you shall see me. See how I go before her! So you should do, sweet Miles.

"She, for her own part, is a woman who doesn't care what man can do to her in the way of honesty and good manners.

"So farewell, fair Mistress Audrey; farewell, Master Miles. I have brought you thus far onward on your way. I must go back now to make clean the rooms where my good lady has been.

"Please commend me to bridegroom Clay and tell him to bear up stiff."

"Stiff" has a bawdy meaning in addition to the meaning of "steadfast."

"Thank you, good Hannibal Puppy," Miles Metaphor said. "I shall fit the leg of your commands with the strait buskins of dispatch very quickly."

"Strait buskins" are tightly fitting coverings for feet and legs.

"Farewell, fine Metaphor," Ball Puppy said.

He exited.

Miles Metaphor said to Audrey, "Come, gentle mistress, will you please to walk?"

"I don't love to be led," Audrey said. "I'd go alone."

Miles Metaphor said, "Let not the mouse of my good meaning, lady, be snapped up in the trap of your suspicion, to lose the tail (or tale) there, either of her truth, or swallowed by the cat of misconstruction."

In this culture, people thought that mice could escape traps by leaving behind their tail.

"You are too finical — too affected — for me," Audrey said. "Speak plainly, sir."

Squire Tub and Basket Hilts entered the scene.

"Welcome again, my Audrey, welcome, love!" Squire Tub said. "You shall go with me; in faith, deny me not. I cannot brook and endure the second hazard, mistress."

"Forbear, Squire Tub," Audrey said. "Stop. As my own mother says, I am not for your mowing. You'll be flown before I am fledged."

One meaning of "mow" is "have sex with."

Squire Tub was older than Audrey. Metaphorically, Audrey was saying that Squire Tub would have flown away from the nest before she had grown the feathers that would enable her to fly.

Since Squire Tub had a tutor and protector in Basket Hilts, and since his mother was so protective of him, however, he may not have been much older than Audrey. She may have been using age as an excuse for not being interested in him.

"Have thou the money, Miles?" Basket Hilts asked.

"Here are two bags," Miles Metaphor said. "Here's fifty pounds in each bag."

Squire Tub said, "Nay, Audrey, I possess you for this time."

He gave Miles Metaphor and Basket Hilts the money and said, "Sirs, take that coin between you and divide it."

He then said to Audrey, "My pretty sweeting, give me now the leave to challenge — claim — love and marriage at your hands."

Audrey said:

"Now out upon you. Aren't you ashamed?

"What will my lady say? Indeed, I think she was at our house, and I think she asked for you, and I think she hit me in the teeth with you — that is, she reproached me about you.

"I thank Her Ladyship, and I think she means not to go away from here until she has found you."

Squire Tub asked, "What are you saying? Was then my lady mother at your house?"

He then said, "Let's have a word with you aside, in private."

"Yes, twenty words," Audrey said.

Tub and Audrey talked together apart from the others.

Lady Tub and Pol-Marten arrived on the scene.

Lady Tub said:

"It is strange, a motion — an impulse — but I know not what, comes into my mind, to leave the way to Totten Court and turn my journey to Kentish Town again.

"And look! Pol-Marten, my son is with his Audrey!

"A while ago, we left her at her father's house, and has he thence removed her in such haste!

"What shall I do? Shall I speak fair words to him, or chide him?"

Pol-Marten advised, "Madam, your worthy son with duteous care can govern his affections. So then, break off their conversation some other way, pretending ignorance of what you know."

Kneeling before Audrey, Squire Tub said to her, "If this is all, fair Audrey, I am thine."

He felt that he could overcome any objections she had to their marriage.

Lady Tub approached him and said, "Mine you were once, though scarcely now your own."

"By God's eyelid, my lady, my lady!" Basket Hilts said.

"Is this my lady bright?" Miles Metaphor asked.

"Madam, you took me now a little tardy — you surprised me," Squire Tub said, rising from his knees.

Lady Tub said:

"At prayers I think you were. What, are you so devout lately that you will shrive you — confess your sins — to all confessors you meet by chance?

"Come, go with me, good Squire, and leave your linen."

Audrey was dressed in linen for her wedding, if it should occur.

Lady Tub was wearing velvet, and velvet is more expensive than linen.

Lady Tub continued:

"I have now some business, which is of some importance, to impart to you."

"Madam, please, spare me just an hour," Squire Tub said. "May it please you to walk before me, and I will follow you."

"It must be now," Lady Tub said. "My business lies this way."

Squire Tub said, "Won't you excuse me until an hour from now, madam?"

Lady Tub said:

"Squire, these excuses argue more your guilt. You have some new plan now to project that the poor tileman — John Clay — scarcely will thank you for.

"What? Will you go?"

Squire Tub said, "I have taken a charge upon me to see this maiden conducted to her father, who with the Chanon Hugh waits for her at Pancras, to see her married to the same John Clay."

Lady Tub said, "It is very well, but Squire, don't you worry about that. I'll send Pol-Marten with her for that office. You shall go along with me — it is decided."

"I have a little business with a friend, madam," Squire Tub said.

Lady Tub replied, "That friend shall wait for you, or you for him."

She then said, "Pol-Marten, take the maiden into your care. Commend me to her father."

"I will follow you," Squire Tub said.

"Tut, don't talk to me about following," Lady Tub said.

"I'll but speak a word," Squire Tub said.

Lady Tub said:

"No whispering; you forget yourself, and you make your love too palpable and obvious.

"A squire, and think so meanly? Fall upon a cow-shard?"

A cow-shard is cow dung.

A proverb stated, "The beetle flies over many a sweet flower and lights on a cow-shard."

Lady Tub continued:

"You know my mind. Come, I'll go to Tobias Turf's house and look for Dido and our Valentine."

Their Valentine was Ball Puppy.

Then she ordered:

"Pol-Marten, look after your charge; I'll look after mine."

Everyone except Pol-Marten and Audrey exited.

Pol-Marten said to himself:

"I smile to think that after so many offers of marriage this maiden has had, she now should fall to me, so that I should have her in my custody!

"It would be but a mad trick to make the attempt, and jump — make — a match with her immediately.

"She's fair and handsome, and she's rich enough. Both time and place provide a fair opportunity to do so.

"Have at it then! I'll do it!"

He asked Audrey, "Fair lady, can you love?"

"No, sir," Audrey answered. "What's that?"

"A toy that women use," Pol-Marten said.

A proverb stated, "Love is a toy [trifle]."

"If it is a toy, it's good to play with," Audrey said.

The noun "toy" can mean amorous activity such as flirtation.

"We will not stand talking about the toy," Pol-Marten said. "The way is short. Does it please you to prove it — to try it — mistress?"

"If you do mean to stand so long upon it, I ask you to let me give it a short cut, sir," Audrey said.

A shortcut is a short way.

A cut is a vulva. Because a vulva consists of the labia (the cut) and the mound of Venus (no cut), aka *mons veneris*, the cut is a short cut.

The verb "stand" can mean to have an erection, which can be another kind of toy.

"It's thus, fair maid: Are you disposed to marry?" Pol-Marten asked.

"You are disposed to ask," Audrey said.

"Are you disposed to grant?" Pol-Marten asked.

"Now I see you are disposed indeed," Audrey said.

"Disposed" can mean "inclined to jest."

Pol-Marten said to himself, "I see that the wench lacks just a little wit and intelligence, and that defect her wealth may well supply."

Actually, Audrey had made a good pun. She understood him quite well.

He then asked out loud, "In plain terms, tell me, will you have me, Audrey?"

Audrey replied:

"In as plain terms, I tell you who would have me.

"John Clay would have me, but he has too-hard — and two hard — hands. I don't like him; besides, he is a thief.

"And Justice Bramble, he would eagerly have catched me and made me his wife.

"But the young Squire, he, rather than his life, would have me yet and make me a lady, he says, and be my knight to do me true knight's service, before his lady mother.

"Can you make me a lady, if I were to have and marry you?"

No, he could not give her the social status of being a lady.

What could he give her?

Pol-Marten said, "I can give you a silken gown and a rich petticoat, and a French hood."

He then said to himself, "All fools love to be brave — splendid. I find her humor, and I will pursue it."

Her humor — personal desire — was to be splendidly dressed. So Pol-Marten thought.

But Audrey did not want to be a lady, and so she was resistant to marrying Squire Tub.

They exited.

Lady Tub, Dame Turf, Squire Tub, and Basket Hilts talked together in the Turfs' house.

Lady Tub said:

"And as I told thee, she was intercepted by the Squire here, my son, and this bold Ruffin, his serving-man, who safely would have carried her to her father and the Chanon Hugh.

"But for more care of the security, my usher has her now in his grave charge."

"Ruffin" is a name for a devil; it also means "ruffian."

Squire Tub's serving-man was Basket Hilts.

Lady Tub's usher was Pol-Marten.

Dame Turf said:

"Now on my faith and halidom, we are beholden to Your Worship."

"Halidom" is something held to be sacred.

She continued:

"She's a girl, a foolish girl, and soon may be tempted. But if this day should pass well once over her head, I'll wish her trust to herself and be responsible for herself, for I have been a very — a true — mother to her, though I am the one who says it."

Some things such as praise of oneself are better said by someone else.

Squire Tub said, "Madam, it is late, and Pancridge is in your way. I think Your Ladyship forgets yourself."

Lady Tub said:

"Your mind runs much on Pancridge. You think a lot about it.

"Well, young Squire, the black ox never trod yet on your foot — adversity has not yet tested you. These idle fancies will forsake you one day."

She then said:

"Come, Mistress Turf, will you go take a walk over the fields to Pancridge, to your husband?"

Dame Turf answered:

"Madam, I would have been there an hour ago, except that I waited on my serving-man, Ball Puppy."

She called:

"What, Ball, I say!"

She then said:

"I think the idle slouch has fallen asleep in the barn, he stays away so long."

Terrified, Ball Puppy entered the scene and said:

"Satin, in the name of velvet Satin, dame!"

By "Satin," he meant, "Satan."

Ball Puppy continued:

"The devil! Oh, the devil is in the barn!

"Help, help! A legion — spirit Legion is in the barn! In every straw is a devil!"

"Legion" with a capital L is the name of a devil; "legion" with a small l is a large number.

"Why do thou bawl so, Puppy?" Dame Turf asked. "Speak, what ails thee?"

He replied, "My name's Ball Puppy, and I bawl. I have seen the devil among the straw. Oh, for a cross, a collop of Friar Bacon, or a conjuring stick of Doctor Faustus! Spirits are in the barn."

A "collop" is a slice of bacon.

Friar Bacon and Doctor Faustus were famous magicians.

"What!" Squire Tub said. "Spirits in the barn? Basket, go and see."

Basket Hilts replied:

"Sir, if you were my master ten times over, and Squire as well, as I already know you are, then you shall pardon me.

"Send me among devils? I zee you love me not.

"Hell be at their game, I'll not trouble them."

"Go and see," Squire Tub said. "I warrant thee there's no such matter."

"If they were giants, it would be another matter," Basket Hilts said. "But devils! No, if I should be torn in pieces, what is your warrant worth? I'll see the fiend set fire to the barn before I come there."

"Now all zaints bless us, if he should be there!" Dame Turf said. "He is an ugly sprite, I warrant."

Ball Puppy said:

"As ugly as any sprite that ever held flesh-hook, dame, or handled fire-fork, rather."

Devils often carried long hooks or forks. Flesh-hooks could be used for hanging the flesh of sinners; fire-forks were used for stirring the fire.

Ball Puppy continued:

"They have put me in a sweet pickle, dame. Except that my lady Valentine smells of musk, I should be ashamed to press into this presence."

In other words: Lady Tub's perfume covers up the stink in his pants that has resulted from his great fear.

"Basket, please, see what is the miracle!" Lady Tub said.

Squire Tub said to Basket Hilts, "Come, go with me. I'll lead. Why stand thou still, man?"

Basket Hilts replied, "Cock's precious, master, you are not mad indeed? You will not go to Hell before your time?"

"Cock's precious" is an oath that has been sanitized for ears that are accustomed to listening for blasphemy. The original oath is "By God's precious blood."

"Why are thou thus afraid?" Squire Tub asked.

"No, not afraid," Basket Hilts said. "But by your leave, I'll come no nearer to the barn."

"Puppy, will thou go with me?" Squire Tub asked.

Ball Puppy said:

"What! Go with you? Whither? Into the barn? Go to whom? The devil? Or to do what there? To be torn among 'hum [them]?

"Wait for my master, the High Constable, or In-and-In, the headborough; let them go into the barn with warrant, seize the fiend, and set him in the stocks for his ill rule.

"It is not for me who am but flesh and blood to meddle with 'un [him]. Vor I cannot, nor I wu'not [and I would not]."

"I pray thee, Tripoly, look and see what is the matter!" Lady Tub said.

Squire Tripoli Tub replied, "That shall I, madam."

He exited.

"May Heaven protect my master!" Basket Hilts said. "I tremble in every joint until he comes back."

Ball Puppy said:

"Now, now, even now the spirits are tearing him in pieces.

"Now are they tossing his legs and arms like they were tossing loggets at a pear-tree."

In a game called loggets, small pieces of wood were thrown near a stake.

The word "pear" can be used to mean vulva, and you can guess what a logget would be. (Parolles uses "pear" to refer to Helena's virgin vulva in Act 1, Scene 1 of William Shakespeare's *All's Well That Ends Well*.)

Ball Puppy continued:

"I'll go to the hole, peep in, and see whether he lives or dies."

"I would not be in my master's coat for thousands of pounds," Basket Hilts said.

In a way, Basket Hilts was wearing his master's coat: He was wearing his master's livery, clothing that identified him as being the servant to a particular master.

Ball Puppy said, "Then pluck it off and turn thyself away."

By taking off his master's livery, Basket Hilts would show that he was quitting his job.

Ball Puppy peeped through a hole and said, "Oh, the devil! The devil! The devil!"

"Where, man? Where?" Basket Hilts asked.

"Alas, that we were ever born!" Dame Turf said. "So near, too!"

They were near to the "devil."

"The Squire has him in his hand, and leads him out by the collar," Ball Puppy said.

Squire Tub led John Clay over to the others.

"Oh, this is John Clay," Dame Turf said.

"John Clay is at Pancras," Lady Tub said. "He is there to be married."

"This was the spirit that reveled in the barn," Squire Tub said.

Ball Puppy said:

"The devil he was! Was this the he [the man] who was crawling among the wheat-straw? Had it been the barley, I should have taken him for the devil in drink, the spirit of the bride-ale!"

Barley is used in making alcoholic beverages: ale and spirits such as brandy.

Ball Puppy continued:

"But poor John, tame John of Clay, that sticks about the bung-hole —"

A bung-hole is a hole in a cask; it is stopped with a bung.

Basket Hilts said:

"If this be all your devil, I would take it in hand to conjure him — I would drive him away.

"But may Hell take me if ever I come in a right — a real — devil's way, if I can keep myself out of it."

"Well meant, Hilts," Squire Tub said.

He exited.

Lady Tub asked, "But how came John Clay thus hid here in the straw, when news was brought to you all that he was at Pancridge, and you believed it?"

Dame Turf answered, "Justice Bramble's serving-man told me so, madam; and by that same token and other things such as a key, he took away my daughter and two sealed bags of money."

"Where's the Squire?" Lady Tub said, not seeing him. "Has he gone away from here?"

"He was here, madam, just now," Dame Turf said.

"Has the hue and cry passed by?" John Clay asked.

"Aye, aye, John Clay," Ball Puppy answered.

"And am I out of danger to be hanged?" John Clay asked.

Robbers could be hanged.

"Hanged, John?" Ball Puppy said. "Yes, to be sure; unless, as with the proverb, you mean to make the choice of your own gallows."

A proverb stated, "If I be hanged, I'll choose my gallows."

"Nay, then all's well," John Clay said. "Hearing your news, Ball Puppy, that you brought from Paddington, I even stole home here, and I thought to hide myself in the barn ever since."

"Oh, wonderful!" Ball Puppy said. "And news was brought us here that you were at Pancridge, ready to be married."

"No, in faith," John Clay said. "I ne'er was furder [further] than the barn."

Dame Turf said:

"Make haste, Puppy! Call forth Mistress Dido Wisp, my lady's gentlewoman, to her lady, and call yourself forth, and a couple of maids, to wait upon me. We are all undone and ruined! My lady is undone! Her fine young son, the Squire, has gotten away."

Dame Turf was afraid that Squire Tub would marry Audrey.

So was Lady Tub, who said to Ball Puppy, "Make haste, haste, good Valentine."

Dame Turf said, "And you, John Clay, you are undone, too! All! My husband is undone, by a true key but a false token; and I myself am undone by parting with my daughter, who'll be married to somebody whom she should not, if we don't make haste."

CHAPTER 5

— 5.1 —

Squire Tub, Pol-Marten, and Audrey talked together.

Squire Tub said, "Please, good Pol-Marten, show thy diligence and faith at the same time. Bring her, but so disguised that the Chanon may not know her and leave me to plot the rest. I will expect thee here."

Pol-Marten replied, "You shall, Squire. I'll perform it with all care, if all my lady's wardrobe will disguise her."

Squire Tub exited.

"Come, Mistress Audrey," Pol-Marten said.

"Has the Squire gone?" Audrey asked.

"He'll meet us by and by, where he appointed," Pol-Marten said. "You shall be splendidly dressed at once so that no one shall know you."

They exited.

Clench, Medley, To-Pan, and D'ogenes Scriben talked together. They were outside Chanon Hugh's house in St. Pancras.

"I wonder where the queen's High Constable is?" Clench said. "I vear they have made 'hun away [carried him away]."

Medley said, "No, zure [to be sure], the Justice dare not conzent to that. He'll zee 'un [him] forthcoming."

In other words: Justice Preamble will make sure that the High Constable appears.

To-Pan said, "He must, vor we can all take corpulent oath that we zaw 'un [him] go in the house."

A corporal oath is ratified by swearing on a Bible or other sacred object.

Scriben said, "Aye, upon record the clock dropped [chimed] twelve at Maribone."

"You are right, D'oge!" Medley said to Scriben. "Zet down to a minute; now it is a'most vour [almost four o'clock]."

Squire Tub and Basket Hilts entered the scene.

"Here comes Squire Tub," Clench said.

"And his governor, Master Basket Hilts," Scriben said. "Do you know 'hun [him]? A valiant wise vellow, az tall a man on his hands as goes on veet."

Scriben was combining two proverbs:

"He is a tall man with his hands." In other words: He is skillful.

"As good a man as ever went on his legs."

Scriben then said, "Bless you, Mas' [Master] Basket."

"Thank you, good D'oge," Basket Hilts said.

"Who's that?" Squire Tub asked.

"D'oge Scriben, the great writer, sir, of Chalcot," Basket Hilts replied.

"And who are the rest?" Squire Tub asked.

Basket Hilts replied, "The wisest heads of the hundred. Medley the joiner, headborough of Islington; Pan of Belsize, and Clench, the leech [physician] of Hampstead: the High Constable's Council, here, of Finsbury."

Squire Tub said, "Prezent me to them, Hilts: Squire Tub of Totten Court."

Basket Hilts said, "Wise men of Finsbury, make place for a squire: I bring to your acquaintance, Tub of Totten Court. Squire Tub, my master, loves all men of virtue, and longs, az one would zay, until he is one of you."

"His Worship's welcun to our company," Clench said. "I wish that our company were even wiser for 'hun [for his sake]!"

To-Pan said, "Here are some of us who are called the witty — that is, wise — men over a hundred —"

Scriben interrupted, "And zome a thousand, when the Muster Day comes."

Muster Day was a day of military parades and inspecting the troops.

Squire Tub said:

"I long, as my man Hilts said, and my governor, to be adopted and accepted into your society.

"Can any man make a masque here in this company?"

"A masque!" To-Pan said. "What's that?"

Scriben answered, "A mumming — a short show, with vizards and fine clothes."

Vizards are masks. Mummings often had disguised characters.

Clench said:

"A disguise, neighbor, is the true word [the older word] for a masque."

He then pointed to Medley and said, "There stands the man who can do it, sir: Medley the joiner, In-and-In of Islington, the only man at a disguize in Middlesex."

In other words: Medley is the only — the best — man in Middlesex for making a masque.

"But who shall write it?" Squire Tub said.

"Scriben, the great writer," Basket Hilts said.

Scriben said:

"In-and-In Medley will do it alone, sir; he will join with no man, although he is a joiner."

In addition to being a carpenter, a joiner can be a collaborator.

Scriben continued:

"In design, as he calls it, he must be sole inventor. In-and-In draws with no other in planning his project, he'll tell you.

"It cannot else be feazible or conduce: Those are his ruling words!

"Will it please you to hear 'hun [him]?"

The verb "conduce" means "bring about a particular result."

Squire Tub said, "Yes. Master In-and-In, I have heard of you."

"I can do nothing, I," Medley said.

"He can do all, sir," Clench said.

"They'll tell you so," Medley said.

Squire Tub said:

"I'd have a toy presented, *A Tale of a Tub*, a story of myself.

"You can express a Tub?"

A toy can be an entertainment, or a trifle.

Medley said, "If it conduce to the design, whatever is feazible. I can express a wash-house, if need be, with a whole pedigree of Tubs."

Squire Tub said, "No, one will be enough to note and give an account of our name and family, Squire Tub of Totten Court, and to show my adventures this very day. I'd have it in Tub's Hall, at Totten Court, my lady mother's house, which is my house indeed, for I am heir to it."

Medley said, "If I might see the place and had surveyed it, I could say more. For all artistic invention, sir, comes by degrees and on the view [consideration] of nature. A world of things concurs to the design, which makes it feazible, if art conduces."

He wanted to see the location of the masque and sketch its layout; such a knowledge of the location could give him ideas on how to present the masque. Such presentations could include mechanical contrivances.

"You say well, witty Master In-and-In," Squire Tub said. "How long have you studied engine?"

The noun "engine" means the making of contrivances; it involves mechanics.

Medley answered, "Since I first joined [first practiced carpentry] or did inlay in wit [using my intelligence], some vorty [forty] years."

"A pretty time!" Squire Tub said.

He then said:

"Basket Hilts, you go and wait on Master In-and-In to Totten Court, and all the other wise masters. Show them the hall and taste the language of the buttery to them."

In other words: Show them the hall and give them a drink.

Squire Tub continued:

"Let them see all the Tub family members about the house, who can talk to him about the matter, until I come — which shall be within an hour at least."

Clench said, "It will be glorious if In-and-In will undertake it, sir. He has a monstrous medley wit of his own."

Squire Tub said:

"Spare for no cost, either in boards or hoops, to architect — design — your tub."

Apparently, a very large tub was planned for the masque.

He continued:

"Haven't you a cooper at London called Vitruvius? Send for him, or old John Heywood, call him to you to help."

Vitruvius was a first-century Roman architect, and John Heywood was an English playwright and musician who went into exile in 1564.

"He scorns the proposal," Scriben said. "Trust to In-and-In Medley alone."

— 5.3 —

Lady Tub, Dame Turf, John Clay, Ball Puppy, and Dido Wisp entered the scene.

Lady Tub said:

"Oh, here's the Squire!

"You slipped away from us finely, son! These manners to your mother will commend you, but in another age, not this.

"Well, Tripoly, your father, good Sir Peter, rest his bones, would not have done this.

"Where's my usher: Pol-Marten? And where is your fair Mistress Audrey?"

"I did not see them," Squire Tub said. "I saw no creature but the four wise masters here of Finsbury Hundred, who came to cry and make public their concern about their constable, Tobias Turf, who they say is lost."

Dame Turf said, "My husband lost! And my fond — foolish — daughter, I fear, is lost, too!

"Where is Pol-Marten, your gentleman, madam?

"Poor John Clay, thou have lost thy Audrey."

"I have lost my wits, my little wits, good mother," John Clay said. "I am distracted and confused."

Ball Puppy said:

"And I have lost my mistress, Dido Wisp, who frowns upon her Puppy, Hannibal."

This kind of mistress is a woman to whom one is devoted; it does not necessarily imply a sexual relationship.

Ball Puppy continued:

"Loss! Loss on every side! A public loss! Loss of my master! Loss of his daughter! Loss of favor, friends, my mistress! Loss of all!"

Justice Preamble and Tobias Turf entered the scene.

"What cry is this?" Justice Preamble asked.

"My serving-man, Ball Puppy, speaks of some loss," Tobias Turf said.

"My master has been found!" Ball Puppy said. "Good luck, if it be thy will, alight on us all!"

"Oh, husband, are you alive?" Dame Turf said. "They said you were lost."

126

"Where's Justice Bramble's clerk?" Tobias Turf asked. "Did he get the money that I sent for?"

"Yes, two hours ago," Dame Turf said. "He got two bags of fifty pounds each in silver, and Audrey, too."

"Why Audrey?" Tobias Turf said. "Who sent for her?"

"You, Master Turf, the fellow said," Dame Turf answered.

"He lied," Tobias Turf said. "I am cozened and cheated, robbed, undone, ruined! Miles Metaphor, your serving-man, is a thief, and has run away with my daughter, Master Bramble, and with my money."

"Neighbor Turf, have patience; I can assure you that your daughter is safe," Lady Tub said. "But as for the money, I know nothing about that."

"My money is my daughter, and my daughter, she is my money, madam," Tobias Turf said.

"I do wonder how your Ladyship has come to know anything in these affairs," Justice Preamble said.

Lady Tub said, "Yes, Justice Bramble, I met the maiden in the fields by chance in the company of the Squire, my son. How he alighted upon — found — her, he himself best can tell."

Squire Tub said, "I intercepted her as she was coming hither to her father, who sent for her by Miles Metaphor, Justice Preamble's clerk. And if Your Ladyship hadn't hindered it, I would have paid back fine Master Justice for his newly made warrant, and for the new pursuivant he served it by this morning."

"Do you know that, sir?" Justice Preamble asked.

Lady Tub said, "You told me, Squire, quite another tale, but I didn't believe you, which made me send Audrey another way by my Pol-Marten, and take my journey back to Kentish Town, where we found John Clay hidden in the barn in order to escape the hue and cry after him; and here he is."

Tobias Turf said:

"John Clay again! Then set cock-a-hoop!"

"Set cock-a-hoop!" means "Let's celebrate!" The cock (tap) of a beer or wine cask would be opened so the liquor would flow freely.

He continued:

"I have lost no daughter, nor no money, Justice.

"John Clay shall pay; I'll look to you now, John. Vaith, out it must, as good at night as morning."

John Clay had broken his bail by escaping, and now Tobias Turf would make him pay back the money that Tobias Turf had spent because John Clay had escaped: one hundred pounds.

Tobias Turf continued:

"I am even as vull [full] as a piper's bag with joy, or a great gun upon carnation [malapropism for 'coronation'] day!

"I could weep lion's tears — huge tears — to see you, John.

"It is but two bags of vifty pounds each I have ventured for you, but now I have you, you shall pay the whole hundred.

"Run from your borrows, son!"

In other words: Tobias Turf was shocked that John Clay had run from the pledges he had made to get Tobias Turf to stand — guarantee — his bail. Those pledges included not running away.

Tobias Turf continued:

"Faith, even be hanged, if you once earth yourself and hide in a hole, John, in the barn, then I have no daughter vor you."

He then asked:

"Who did verret 'hun [ferret John Clay out]?"

Dame Turf answered, "My lady's son, the Squire here, vetched 'hun [him] out. Puppy had put us all in such a vright [fright] that we thought the devil was in the barn, and nobody dared to venture against hun [him]."

"I have now resolved who shall have my daughter," Tobias Turf said.

"Who?" Dame Turf asked.

"He who best deserves her," Tobias Turf said.

That person could be Squire Tub, who had shown courage in going into the barn when others thought that at least one devil was inside.

Seeing Chanon Hugh coming, Tobias Turf said, "Here comes the vicar."

He then said to him, "Chanon Hugh, we have vound John Clay again! The matter's all come round."

"Has Miles Metaphor returned yet?" Chanon Hugh asked.

"All is turned here to confusion, and we have lost our plot," Justice Preamble said. "I fear my serving-man has run away with the money, and John Clay has been found, in whom old Tobias Turf is sure to save his stake."

"What shall we do then, Justice?" Chanon Hugh asked.

"The bride was met in the young Squire's hands," Justice Preamble said.

"And what's become of her?" Chanon Hugh asked.

"None here can tell," Justice Preamble said.

"Wasn't my mother's serving-man, Pol-Marten, with you, and a strange gentlewoman in his company, recently here, Chanon?" Squire Tub asked.

"Yes, and I dispatched them," Chanon Hugh said.

"Dispatched them!" Squire Tub said. "What do you mean?"

"Why, I married them, as they desired, just now," Chanon Hugh said.

"And do you know what you have done, Sir Hugh?" Squire Tub asked.

"No harm, I hope," Chanon Hugh said.

Squire Tub said, "You have ended all the quarrel: Audrey is married."

He had guessed the truth: The strange gentlewoman who had gotten married to Pol-Marten was Audrey, dressed in fine clothing.

"Married! To whom?" Lady Tub asked.

"My daughter Audrey married, and she not know of it!" Tobias Turf said.

Certainly, no one had anticipated the marriage: Apparently, no one, including Audrey, had ever thought that Pol-Marten would be her groom.

"Nor her father or mother!" Dame Turf said.

"Whom has she married?" Lady Tub asked

"Your Pol-Marten, madam," Squire Tub said. "A groom who was never dreamt of."

"Is he a man?" Tobias Turf asked.

"That he is, Turf," Lady Tub said, "and I have made him a gentleman."

Pol-Marten was her gentleman-usher.

"If he is a gentleman, then let Audrey shift for herself," Dame Turf said.

If Audrey had married a gentleman, she had married well, and yes, she could look after herself.

Chanon Hugh said:

"She was so bravely — splendidly — dressed, I didn't know who she was, I swear. And yet as a vicar I officiated at the wedding and married her by her own name to him.

"But she was so disguised, so ladylike, I think she did not know herself the while!

"I married them to each other as if they were a complete pair of strangers to me, and they presented themselves to me as such."

"I wish them much joy, as they have given me heart's ease," Lady Tub said.

She was relieved that her son had not married Audrey.

Squire Tub said, "Then, madam, I'll entreat you now to relinquish your anxiety about and mistrust of me, and please to take all this good company home with you to supper. We'll have a merry night of it and laugh."

Lady Tub said:

"That is a very good proposal, Squire, which I yield to and grant and thank them to accept my invitation.

"Neighbor Turf, I'll have you and your wife be merry, and you, Sir Hugh, shall be pardoned for this your happy error by Justice Preamble, your friend and patron."

"If the young Squire can pardon it, then so do I," Justice Preamble said.

Most of them exited.

— 5.5 —

Ball Puppy, Dido Wisp, and Chanon Hugh tarried behind.

Ball Puppy said:

"Stay, my dear Dido.

"Good Vicar Hugh, we have some business with you.

"In short, this: If you dare knit another pair of strangers, Dido of Carthage and her countryman, stout Hannibal, stand to it. I have asked consent to marry her, and she has granted me her consent."

"Stands to it" means that he is ready to be married; the phrase also has a bawdy meaning.

"But does Dido say so?" Chanon Hugh asked.

Dido Wisp replied, "I dare not demur from what Ball Hanny has said."

"Come in then," Chanon Hugh said. "I'll dispatch you and marry you to each other. A good supper, good company, good discourse would not be lost, and above all, a place and time where wit has any source."

They exited.

Pol-Marten, Audrey, Squire Tub, and Lady Tub talked together at Totten Court.

Pol-Marten said, "After the hoping of your pardon, madam, for many faults committed, here my wife and I do stand, awaiting your mild judgment and sentence on us."

"I wish thee joy, Pol-Marten, and thy wife as much, Mistress Pol-Marten," Lady Tub said. "Thou have tricked — dressed — her up in very fine clothing, I think."

"For that I made bold with Your Ladyship's wardrobe, but I have trespassed within the limits of your leave — I hope," Pol-Marten said.

Lady Tub said:

"I give her what she wears; I know that all women love to be finely dressed.

"Thou have deserved it of me: I am extremely pleased with thy good fortune."

Justice Preamble, Tobias Turf, Dame Turf, and John Clay entered the scene.

Lady Tub said:

"Welcome, good Justice Preamble.

"Tobias Turf, look merrily on your daughter: She has married a gentleman."

"So I think," Tobias Turf said. "I dare not touch her, she is so fine; yet I will say, God bless her!"

If she were not so very well dressed, he would give her a hug and kiss to celebrate her marriage.

"And I, too, my fine daughter!" Dame Turf said. "I could love her now twice as well as if John Clay had married her."

Squire Tub said:

"Come, come, my mother is pleased. I pardon all.

"Pol-Marten, come in, and wait upon my lady.

"Welcome, good guests!

"See that supper is served in with all the plenty of the house and with all respect and ceremony.

"I must confer with Master In-and-In Medley about some alterations in my masque.

"Send Basket Hilts out to me; tell him to bring the Council of Finsbury hither.

"I'll have such a night that shall make the name of Totten Court immortal and be recorded to posterity."

Everyone except Squire Tub exited.

In-and-In Medley, Clench, To-Pan, and Scriben entered the scene.

"Oh, Master In-and-In, what have you done about the masque?" Squire Tub said.

In-and-In Medley said:

"Surveyed the place, sir, and designed the layout or starting point of the work; and this it is.

"First, I have fixèd in the earth a tub, and an old tub, like a saltpeter tub, preluding by [malapropism for 'alluding to'] your father's name, Sir Peter, and the antiquity of your house and family, originating from saltpeter."

"Good, in faith," Squire Tub said. "You have shown reading about and proper knowledge of our family history here, sir."

"I have a little knowledge in design, which I can vary, sir, to *infinito* [to infinity, aka indefinitely]," Medley said.

"*Ad infinitum*, sir, you mean," Squire Tub said.

Ad infinitum is Latin; *infinito* is Italian.

Medley said:

"I do. I stand not on my Latin; I don't know Latin well.

"I'll invent, but I must be alone then, joined with no man. This we call the stand-still — starting point and foundation — of our work."

"Who are those 'we' you now joined to yourself?" Squire Tub asked.

"I mean myself still, in the plural number," Medley said, "And out of this we raise our *Tale of a Tub*."

Squire Tub said:

"No, Master In-and-In, my *Tale of a Tub*.

"By your leave, I am Tub: the tale is about me and my adventures! I am Squire Tub, *subjectum fabulae* — the subject of our story."

"But I am the author," Medley said.

Squire Tub said:

"The workman, sir! The artificer, I grant you."

An artificer is 1) a skilled craftsman, and/or 2) a trickster.

He continued:

"So John Skelton the laureate was the artificer of *Elinour Bumming*, but she was the subject of the rout and tunning."

A rout is a fuss, and tunning means pouring liquor into a large beer or wine cask.

Skelton's poem was actually titled *The Tunning of Elinor Rumming*.

"He has put you to it, neighbor In-and-In," Clench said. "He has caught you out."

"Do not dispute with him," To-Pan said. "He who pays for all will always win."

Scriben asked, "Are you revised [malapropism for 'advised'] of that? Are you sure of that? A man may have wit and intelligence, and yet take off his hat to show respect to someone else."

Medley continued his description of what he had created for the masque:

"Now, sir, this tub I will have capped — topped — with paper, a fine oiled lantern paper that we use."

"Yes, every barber, every cutler has it," To-Pan said.

Medley said:

"Which in the tub does contain the light to the business and shall with the very vapor of the candle drive all the motions of our matter about, as we present them."

The device was a large tub or barrel that lay on its side with a candle and puppets inside. The candlelight cast shadows of the puppets on the fine oiled lantern paper, which allowed the shadows to be seen. The candlelight also flickered, causing the puppets to seem to move.

"Motions" are puppets; the "matter" was the entertainment.

Medley continued:

"For example, first the Worshipful Lady Tub —"

Squire Tub interrupted: "Right Worshipful, please; I am Worshipful myself."

Lady Tub had a title superior to his, and so she was entitled to be called "Right Worshipful."

Medley said:

"Your Squireship's mother passes by — her usher Master Pol-Marten, bare-headed before her — in her velvet gown."

Squire Tub asked, "But how shall the spectators, as it might be I, or Hilts, know it is my mother? Or that it is Pol-Marten, there, who walks before her?"

"Oh, we do nothing if we do not make that clear," Medley said.

He did not explain how that would be made clear.

"You have seen none of his works, sir," Clench said to Squire Tub.

To-Pan mentioned one of Medley's works: "All the postures — positions at drill — of the trained bands of citizen-soldiers of the country, aka county."

"All their colors — their banners," Scriben added.

"And all their captains," To-Pan added.

"All the cries of the city, and all the trades in their liveries," Clench added.

Scriben said:

"He has his whistle of command, seat of authority, and virge — rod of office — to interpret [explain his purpose], tipped with silver, sir!

"You don't know him and how excellent he is."

Medley would use a whistle to give commands concerning the masque.

"Well, I will leave it all to him," Squire Tub said.

"Give me the brief — the abstract — of your subject. Leave the whole state of the thing to me," Medley said.

Basket Hilts entered the scene and said, "Supper is ready, sir. My Lady calls for you."

"I'll send the brief to you in writing," Squire Tub said to Medley.

"Sir, I will render feazible and facile — practicible and easy to accomplish — what you expect," Medley promised.

Squire Tub said:

"Hilts, let it be your responsibility to see the wise of Finsbury made welcome. Let them lack nothing.

"Has old Rosin been sent for?"

"He's come and is inside," Basket Hilts said.

Squire Tub went inside.

"Lord, what a world of business the Squire dispatches!" Scriben said.

"He is a learned man," Medley said. "I think there are only a vew [few] who are of the Inns of Court or the Inns of Chancery like him."

The Inns of Court and the Inns of Chancery were legal associations and institutions.

"Let's take care to do what he needs," Clench said.

Everyone exited except Basket Hilts.

— 5.8 —

Black Jack, Lady Tub's butler, walked over to Basket Hilts and said, "Yonder's another wedding couple, Master Basket, brought in by Vicar Hugh."

"Who are they, Jack?" Basket Hilts asked.

"The High Constable's serving-man, Ball Hanny, and Mistress Wisp, our lady's serving-woman," Black Jack said.

"And are the table merry?" Basket Hilts asked.

"There's a young tile-maker who makes all laugh," Black Jack said. "He will not eat his food, but cries at the table that he shall be hanged."

Of course, he was in no danger of being hanged. The robbery he had been accused of committing was a lie: It never happened.

"He has lost his wench already," Basket Hilts said. "He might as well be hanged."

"Was the mistress — loved one — of Pol-Marten, our fellow servant, the wench intended for that sneak-John?" Black Jack asked.

"Sneak-John" is John Clay, whom Black Jack regards as shifty.

Basket Hilts said:

"Indeed, Black Jack, he should have been her bridegroom.

"But I must go to wait on my wise masters.

"Jack, you shall wait on me, and see the masque soon; I am half Lord Chamberlain in my master's absence."

The Lord Chamberlain arranged entertainments such as masques for the royal court.

"Shall we have a masque?" Black Jack asked. "Who makes it?"

Basket Hilts replied:

"In-and-In Medley, the maker — craftsman — of Islington.

"Come, go with me to the sage sentences — the sages who provide wise judgment — of Finsbury."

They exited.

Two servants prepared a room for the masque by setting out chairs for the audience.

"Come, bring in the great chair for my lady," the first servant said, "and set it there, and set out this chair for Justice Bramble."

"This chair is for the Squire, my master, on the right hand," the second servant said.

"And this chair is for the High Constable," the first servant said.

"This chair is for his wife," the second servant said.

"Then here are chairs for the bride and bridegroom," the first servant said. "Here is Pol-Marten's chair."

"And the chair for she Pol-Marten is at my lady's feet," the second servant said.

"Right," the first servant said.

"And beside them is the chair for Master Hannibal Puppy," the second servant said.

"And his she-Puppy, Mistress Wisp who was," the first servant said. "Here's all the chairs that are mentioned in the note."

The second servant said, "No, a chair is also needed for Master Vicar, the petty Chanon Hugh."

In Chanon Hugh's case, "petty" means 1) a minor cleric, and 2) small-minded.

"And a chair is needed for cast-by — rejected — John Clay," the first servant said.

They finished setting out the chairs, and the first servant said, "There are all the chairs that are needed."

Squire Tub entered the room and said:

"Cry, 'A hall! A hall!'

"It is merry in Tottenham Hall, when beards wag all."

The cry "A hall! A hall!" meant "Clear space for an entertainment!"

Squire Tub then called, "Come, Father Rozin, with your fiddle now, and two tall — fine — tooters. Play a flourish to announce the masque!"

The musicians entered and played a flourish.

Justice Preamble entered the hall, followed by Lady Tub, Tobias Turf, Dame Turf, Pol-Marten, Audrey, Puppy, Wisp, Chanon Hugh, John Clay, and the Council of Finsbury: In-and-In Medley, Scriben, To-Pan, and Clench.

All took their seats. Basket Hilts stood off to the side. His job was to cry "Peace!" aka "Silence!" before each episode of the masque.

Lady Tub said:

"Neighbors, all are welcome! Now Totten Hall looks like a court, and hence shall first be called so."

The name would be Totten Court, aka Tottenham Court.

Lady Tub continued:

"Your witty short confession, Master Vicar, which you gave in another room, has been the prologue, and has revealed much to my son's device, his *Tale of a Tub*."

"Let my masque show itself, and In-and-In, the architect, appear," Squire Tub said. "I hear the whistle."

In-and-In Medley was blowing the whistle to announce that the masque was ready to start.

Basket Hilts said loudly, "Peace! Let there be silence!"

In-and-In Medley appeared in front of the curtain that the stage had in front. He would give brief descriptions of each episode of the masque.

Medley read the introduction of the masque out loud:

"*Thus rise I first, in my light linen breeches,*

"*To run the meaning over in short speeches.*

"*Here is a tub: a Tub of Totten Court,*

"*An ancient Tub, has called you to this sport [entertainment].*

"*His father was a knight, the rich Sir Peter,*

"*Who got his wealth by a tub and by saltpeter,*

"*And left all to his Lady Tub, the mother*

"*Of this bold Squire Tub, and to no other.*

"*Now of this Tub and's [and his] deeds, not done in ale,*

"*Observe, and you shall see the very tale.*"

In other words: Squire Tub was not drunk when he did these deeds; this Tub did not contain ale.

In-and-In Medley then drew the curtain and revealed the top of the tub.

Basket Hilts said loudly, "Peace! Let there be silence!"

Music played to announce the first episode of the masque.

For each motion, or episode, of the masque, candlelight cast the shadows of the puppets onto oiled lantern paper, and Medley read out loud a poem that interpreted what the audience was seeing.

Medley read the first episode of the masque out loud:

"*Here Chanon Hugh first brings to Totten Hall*

"*The High Constable's counsel, tells the Squire all;*

"*Which, though discovered [revealed] — give the devil his due —*

"*The wise [men] of Finsbury do still pursue.*

"*Then with the Justice doth [does] he [Chanon Hugh] counterplot,*

"*And his clerk, Metaphor, to cut that knot [prevent that marriage];*

"*Whilst Lady Tub, in her sad [dark-colored] velvet gown,*

"*Missing her son, doth [does] seek him up and down.*"

"With her Pol-Marten bare-headed before her," Squire Tub said.

Medley said, "Yes, I have expressed it here in the shadow-figure, and Mistress Wisp, her woman, holding up her train."

"In the next page report your second strain — the second part of your poem," Squire Tub said.

Basket Hilts said loudly, "Peace! Let there be silence!"

Music sounded.

Medley read the second episode of the masque out loud:

"*Here the High Constable and sages walk*

"*To church. The dame, the daughter, bride-maids talk*

"*Of wedding-business, till a fellow in comes,*

"*Relates the robbery of one Captain Thumbs;*

"*Chargeth the bridegroom with it, troubles all,*

"*And gets the bride; who in the hands doth [does] fall*

"*Of the bold Squire, but thence soon is ta'en [taken]*

"*By the sly Justice and his clerk profane,*

"*In shape [disguise] of pursuivant; which he not long*

"*Holds, but betrays all with his trembling tongue;*

"*As truth will break out and show —*"

The "clerk profane" is Miles Metaphor, who is a civil clerk and not a clerk in holy orders.

Squire Tub interrupted, looking at the shadow-figures, "Oh, thou have made him kneel there in a corner, I see now. There is simple — sterling — honor for you, Hilts!"

Basket Hilts had knocked Miles Metaphor down.

Miles Metaphor's cowardice is also mentioned in episode four of the masque.

"Didn't I make him confess all to you?" Basket Hilts asked.

Squire Tub replied, "True, In-and-In has done you right, you see."

He then requested, "Thy third part of the poem, please, witty In-and-In."

Clench said, "The Squire commends 'un [him: In-and-In Medley]; he likes all well."

"He cannot choose not to," To-Pan said. "This is gear made to sell — it is good."

Basket Hilts said loudly, "Peace! Let there be silence!"

Music sounded.

Medley read the third episode of the masque out loud:

"*The careful [troubled] Constable here drooping comes,*

"*In his deluded search [he has been fooled into making the search] of [that is, for] Captain Thumbs.*

"*Puppy brings word his daughter's run away*

"*With the tall [valiant] serving-man [Basket Hilts]. He frights [frightens] groom Clay*

"*Out of his wits. Returneth then the Squire,*

"*Mocks all their pains, and gives fame out a liar [shows that the report is a lie]*

"*For falsely charging Clay, when 'twas [it was] the plot*

"*Of subtle Bramble, who had Audrey got*

"*Into his hand by this winding [devious] device.*

"*The father makes a rescue in a trice,*

"*And with his daughter, like Saint George on foot,*

"*Comes home triumphing to his dear heart root [to his beloved wife];*

"*And tells the Lady Tub, whom he meets there,*

"*Of her son's courtesies [courting of Audrey], the bachelor,*

"Whose words had made 'em fall [that is, made them give up] the hue and cry.
"When Captain Thumbs coming to ask him why
"He had so done, he cannot yield him cause,
"But so he runs his neck into the laws [he becomes caught up in legal trouble]."

Basket Hilts said loudly, "Peace! Let there be silence!"

Music sounded.

Medley read the fourth episode of the masque out loud:

"The laws, who have a noose to crack his neck,
"As Justice Bramble tells him, who doth [does] peck
"A hundred pounds out of his purse, that comes
"Like his teeth from him, unto Captain Thumbs."

A proverb stated, "To get money from him is like pulling teeth."

Medley continued reading the fourth episode of the masque out loud:

"Thumbs is the Vicar in a false disguise,
"And employs Metaphor to fetch this prize,
"Who tells the secret unto Basket Hilts,
"For fear of beating. This the Squire quilts [that is, stitches together]
"Within his cap, and bids him but purloin [steal]
"The wench for him; they two shall share the coin.
"Which the sage lady [Lady Tub] in her 'foresaid gown
"Breaks off, returning unto Kentish Town
"To seek her Wisp, taking the Squire along,
"Who finds Clay John, as hidden in straw throng [in tightly pressed, aka thick, straw]."

Basket Hilts said:

"Oh, how I am beholden to the inventor, who would not, on record against me, write about my slackness here to enter the barn!

"Well, In-and-In, I see thou can discern!"

Squire Tub said to Medley, "Go on with your last episode, and come to a conclusion."

Basket Hilts said loudly, "Peace! Let there be silence!"

Music sounded.

Medley read the fifth and final episode of the masque out loud:

"The last is known, and needs but small infusion [pouring]
"Into your memories, by leaving in

"*These figures as you sit [by letting the puppets remain still, just as the audience members whom the puppets represent are sitting still]. I, In-and-In,*

"*Present you with the show: first, of a Lady*

"*Tub and her son, of whom this masque here made I.*

"*Then bridegroom Pol and Mistress Pol the bride,*

"*With the sub-couple, who sit them beside [sit beside them].*"

The sub-couple were Ball Puppy and Dido Wisp.

Squire Tub said, "That is the only verse I altered for the better, *euphonia gratia.*"

Euphonia gratia is supposed to mean "for the sake of euphony," but the correct Latin phrase is *euphoniae gratia.*

Medley finished reading the fifth episode out loud:

"*Then Justice Bramble, with Sir Hugh the Chanon,*

"*And the bride's parents, which I will not stan' on [stand on, insist upon],*

"*Or the lost Clay, with the recovered Miles;*

"*Who thus unto his master him 'conciles [reconciles],*

"*On the Squire's word, to pay old Turf his club [pay his contribution — that is, pay the money stolen from him].*

"*And so doth [does] end our Tale, here, of a Tub.*"

EPILOGUE

Squire Tub said to you, the audience:

"This tale of me, the Tub of Totten Court,

"A poet [playwright] first invented for your sport [entertainment],

"Wherein the fortune of most empty tubs,

"Rolling in love, are shown, and with what rubs [difficulties]

"We're [We are] commonly encountered, when the wit [intelligence]

"Of the whole Hundred so opposeth [opposed] it.

"Our petty Chanon's forkèd [devilish] plot in chief,

"Sly Justice's arts, with the High Constable's brief

"And brag [spirited] commands; my lady mother's care [worry, suspicion],

"And her Pol-Marten's fortune; with the rare

"Fate of poor John, thus tumbled in the cask;"

["Poor john" is dried, salted fish that is preserved in a cask.]

[Being in a cask as others roll it would certainly shake up someone, as has metaphorically happened to poor John Clay in this play.]

Squire Tub concluded:

"Got In-and-In to gi't [to present it to] you in a masque:

"That [So that] you be pleased, who came to see a play,

"With those that [who] hear and mark [notice] not what we say.

"Wherein the poet's fortune is, I fear,

"Still [Always] to be early up, but ne'er the near."

[Getting up early and making a good play will not solve the problem of audience members who don't pay attention.]

NOTES

— Cast of Characters —

RASI CLENCH

For Your Information:

NOMAD - How to use clench nails.

This video is about a fastening technique found in wooden boatbuilding called "clench nailing". It's pretty simple and very effective. It is primarily used in small boats but older Pacific commercial fishing craft also employed a variation of the technique.

https://www.youtube.com/watch?v=240NwYVCnew

D'OGENES SCRIBEN

Many Cynics were beggars and the Cynic Diogenes was sometimes called the Dog. The word "Cynic" means "Dog-like."

The Cynics believed in rejecting wealth, fame, and power and instead living a simple life. They often publicly and caustically rejected wealth, fame, and power and the people who pursued them.

Diogenes once carried a lit lamp during the daytime and claimed to be looking for a man — any man — but all he could find were scoundrels. (Retellings of this story sometimes say that he was looking for an honest man.)

Alexander the Great heard about Diogenes, met him, and asked if he could do anything for him. In doing so, Alexander stood between the famous Cynic and the sun and cast a shadow on him. Diogenes replied, "Yes, you can stand out of my sunlight."

Alexander told him, "If I were not Alexander, I would want to be Diogenes." Diogenes replied, "If I were not Diogenes, I would want to be Diogenes."

When Alexander wondered why Diogenes was looking at a pile of bones, Diogenes replied, "I am looking for the bones of your father, but I cannot distinguish them from the bones of his slaves."

HUGH

The beetle and wedges will, where you will have 'em. 25

(1.5.25)

Source of Above:

The Cambridge Edition of the Works of Ben Jonson

7 Volume Set. Volume 6.

Ben Jonson (Author), David Bevington (Editor), Martin Butler (Editor), Ian Donaldson (Editor).

Cambridge University Press, 2012. Print. P. 571.

Here is some information on beetle and wedges:

Old-fashioned terms defined from John Fairfield's 1646 will (Gen. 1: John)

A beetle and fowre wedges

A beetle is a tool resembling a hammer but with a large head (usually wooden); used to drive wedges or ram down paving stones or for crushing or beating or flattening or smoothing. "The beetle and wedge ... a very effective way of splitting large logs for firewood," says an English website. "The beetle is a heavy hammer, and the iron wedges are hammered in to force the log apart, using much less effort than splitting with an axe." Thomas Tusser, who farmed in Suffolk and Essex in the 16th century, published a book, Five Hundred Points of Husbandrie, *in 1573. It contained this verse:*

When frost will not suffer, to dike and to hedge then get thee a heat, with they beetle and wedge:

Once Hallomas come, and a fire by the hall, such slivers do well, for to lie by the wall.

Source of Above:

"Descendants of John Fairfield of Wenham: A genealogy site inspired by the research of Wynn Cowan Fairfield." Accessed 14 May 2022. http://www.fairfieldfamily.com/records/court%20documents/html/oldterms.html

— 2.1 —

I love no trains o' Kent
    Or Christendom, as they say.
    (2.1.37-38)
    Source of Above:
    The Cambridge Edition of the Works of Ben Jonson
    7 Volume Set. Volume 6.
    Ben Jonson (Author), David Bevington (Editor), Martin Butler (Editor),
Ian Donaldson (Editor).
    Cambridge University Press, 2012. Print. P. 578.
    Below is some information about "trains [tails] o' Kent":

Kentish Longtails

BY IAN · PUBLISHED SEPTEMBER 6, 2012 · UPDATED
DECEMBER 10, 2018

The inhabitants of Strood in Kent were once nicknamed Kentish
Longtails. Though this could relate to the belief in medieval
mainland Europe that the English had tails, there is a folk tale
relating a curse placed on the people of Strood by Thomas Becket,
Archbishop of Canterbury.

It is said that whilst Thomas Becket (Born 1118 – Died 29
December 1170) was riding through Strood, a town that supported
King Henry II against the Archbishop, he was waylaid by the
inhabitants and an argument ensued. Robert de Broc, or a nephew
of his cut off the tail of Thomas Becket's horse. The story goes on
to say that the result of this insult was a curse put on the people of
Strood and de Broc, by Thomas Becket, that all their descendants
would be born with tails.

There is an historical account which mentions Robert de Broc, the
cutting off of a horses tail and subsequent excommunication by

Becket. According to William Fitz Stephen (William Fitzstephen) (Died 1191) – Becket's household clerk. *'On Christmas eve he read the lesson from the gospel, "the book of the generation", and celebrated the midnight mass. Before high mass on Christmas day, which he also celebrated, he preached a splendid sermon to the people, taking for his subject a text on which he was wont to ponder, namely, "on earth peace to men of good will". When he made mention of the holy fathers of the church of Canterbury who were therein confessors, he said that they already had one archbishop who was a martyr, St Alphege, and it was possible that they would shortly have another. And because of the shameful injury inflicted on the horse of a certain poor peasant of his, a servant of the church of Canterbury, by cutting off its tail, he bound Robert de Broc with a sentence of excommunication. He had previously threatened him through messengers, while inviting him to make reparation. But Robert, being contumacious, had returned answer by a certain knight, David of Romney, that if the archbishop excommunicated him he would act like an excommunicate. Also, those who had violently taken possession of his two churches of Harrow and Throwley and had refused to admit his officers, he involved in the same sentence.'*

Source: Ian. "Kentish Longtails." *Mysterious Britain and Ireland.* 10 December 2018

https://www.mysteriousbritain.co.uk/folklore/kentish-longtails/

— 2.2 —

Hare the poor fellow out on his five wits,
    And seven senses? (145)
(2.2.144-145)
Source of Above:
The Cambridge Edition of the Works of Ben Jonson
7 Volume Set. Volume 6.
Ben Jonson (Author), David Bevington (Editor), Martin Butler (Editor), Ian Donaldson (Editor).
Cambridge University Press, 2012. Print. P. 585.
Here is some information on the five wits:

Five Wits

In the time of William Shakespeare, there were commonly reckoned to be **five wits** and **five senses**. The five wits were sometimes taken to be synonymous with the five senses, but were otherwise also known and regarded as the **five inward wits**, distinguishing them from the five senses, which were the five *outward* wits.

Much of this conflation has resulted from changes in meaning. In Early Modern English, "wit" and "sense" overlapped in meaning. Both could mean a faculty of perception (although this sense dropped from the word "wit" during the 17th century). Thus "five wits" and "five senses" could describe both groups of wits/senses, the inward and the outward, although the common distinction, where it was made, was "five wits" for the inward and "five senses" for the outward.

The inward and outward wits are a product of many centuries of philosophical and psychological thought, over which the concepts gradually developed, that have their origins in the works of Aristotle. The concept of five outward wits came to medieval thinking from Classical philosophy, and found its most major expression in

151

Christian devotional literature of the Middle Ages. The concept of five inward wits similarly came from Classical views on psychology.

Modern thinking is that there are more than five (outward) senses, and the idea that there are five (corresponding to the gross anatomical features — eyes, ears, nose, skin, and mouth — of many higher animals) does not stand up to scientific scrutiny. (For more on this, see Definition of sense.) But the idea of five senses/wits from Aristotelian, medieval, and 16th century thought still lingers so strongly in modern thinking that a sense beyond the natural ones is still called a "sixth sense".

The "inward" wits

Stephen Hawes' poem *Graunde Amoure* shows that the five (inward) wits were "common wit", "imagination", "fantasy", "estimation", and "memory". "Common wit" corresponds to Aristotle's concept of *common sense* (sensus communis), and "estimation" roughly corresponds to the modern notion of instinct.

Shakespeare himself refers to these wits several times, in *Romeo and Juliet* (Act I, scene 4, and Act II, scene iv), *King Lear* (Act III, scene iv), *Much Ado About Nothing* (Act I, scene i, 55), and *Twelfth Night* (Act IV, scene ii, 92). He distinguished between the five wits and the five senses, as can be seen from Sonnet 141.

Source of Above: "Five Wits." Wikipedia. Accessed 6 June 2022. https://en.wikipedia.org/wiki/Five_wits

The traditional five senses are hearing, sight, touch, taste, and smell, and no doubt the joke here is that Dame Turf has gotten the number wrong.

Two other senses, however, may be balance (vestibular sense) and movement (proprioception).

For Your Information:

Vestibular

*The **vestibular system** explains the perception of our body in relation to gravity, movement and balance. The vestibular system measures acceleration, g-force, body movements and head position. Examples of the vestibular system in practice include knowing that you are moving when you are in an elevator, knowing whether you are lying down or sat up, and being able to walk along a balance beam.*

Proprioception

***Proprioception** is the sense of the relative position of neighbouring parts of the body and strength of effort being employed in movement. This sense is very important as it lets us know exactly where our body parts are, how we are positioned in space and to plan our movements. Examples of our proprioception in practice include being able to clap our hands together with our eyes closed, write with a pencil and apply with correct pressure, and navigate through a narrow space.*

Source: of Above: "What are the 7 Senses?" 7 Senses Foundation. Accessed 6 June 2022.

http://www.7senses.org.au/what-are-the-7-senses/

$$- \mathbf{2.3} -$$

I laugh to think what a fine fool's finger they have
    O'this wise constable, in pricking out
This Captain Thumbs to his neighbors.
(2.3.41-43)
Source of Above:
The Cambridge Edition of the Works of Ben Jonson
7 Volume Set. Volume 6.
Ben Jonson (Author), David Bevington (Editor), Martin Butler (Editor), Ian Donaldson (Editor).
Cambridge University Press, 2012. Print. P. 588.
Below is some information on "fool's finger":

The dully-named *middle finger* was, to our forbears the *fool's finger*, but not, alas, because it was covered in ink. Instead we got the name from the Romans who called it the *digitus infamis* (*infamous*), *obscenus* (*obscene*), and *impudicus* (*rude*). Nobody is sure why the Romans bore such a grudge against the middle finger, but it seems that it was they who invented the habit of sticking it up at those they did not like.

As Martial so delicately put it:

Rideto multum qui te, Sextille, cinaedum

dixerit et digitum porrigito medium

Which translates *extraordinarily* loosely as:

If you are called a poof don't pause or linger

But laugh and show the chap your middle finger.

Source of Above:

"Digital Information and Flipping the Finger." Blog.inkyfool.com. 10 December 2010

https://blog.inkyfool.com/2010/12/digital-information-and-flipping-finger.html

Below is more information about the middle finger:

The middle finger is mostly known from Greek comedy, but it is also mentioned in some Latin sources.

Martial's *Epigram* 28, lines 1–2:

Rideto multum qui te, Sextille, cinaedum

Dixerit et digitum porrigito medium.

"Laugh at the man who calls you a faggot, Sextillus, and extend your middle finger."

And:

Logeion, s.v. *impudicus*, gives Martial 6.70.5 which mind you isn't specified as being the middle finger. But there's an interesting and amusing commentary on that passage in an article (CJ 47:67) on Roman Elementary Mathematics by J. Hilton Turner, which makes it pretty clear that it was. Elsewhere in the same article, there's a translation of a chunk of Bede in which he talks of the middle finger (clear from the context, despite no Latin original in the article) as *impudicus*.

In Muratori (XI, part 3, p126), in the anonymous *Liber de computo sive kalendario* attributed to Cyril of Alexandria, §138 there's another *digitus impudicus*; here too in the context of representing numbers on one's fingers.

Roger Pack, "Catullus, Carmen V: Abacus or Finger-Counting?", AJP 77:47-51 at JSTOR builds on another part of the Turner article, by suggesting that the Catullus poem maybe is best viewed not on an abacus with Turner, but in finger-counting, and there's a bit about the *impudicus* in his article as well.

Source: "Was the middle finger obscene in Ancient Rome?" Accessed 16 May 2022.
https://latin.stackexchange.com/questions/1389/was-the-middle-finger-obscene-in-ancient-rome

<h1 style="text-align:center">— 3.1 —</h1>

Oh, there are two vat pigs
> *A-zindging by the vire, now by Saint Tony,*
> *Too good to eat but on a wedding-day;* 50

(3.1.48-50)

Source of Above:

The Cambridge Edition of the Works of Ben Jonson

7 Volume Set. Volume 6.

Ben Jonson (Author), David Bevington (Editor), Martin Butler (Editor), Ian Donaldson (Editor).

Cambridge University Press, 2012. Print. P. 598.

This is some information about Saint Anthony's association with pigs:

The Possible Connections with Pigs

So what is the connection with St. Anthony and pigs? Here are several various explanations.

The first explanation is that the pig represents evil that St. Anthony had to overcome as he fought the temptations of the world, the flesh, and the devil. Pigs, for obvious reasons, are associated with the ground and the earth. Thus, the idea is that some artists wanted to depict how St. Anthony defeated the earthly temptations by including a pig to represent the worldly sins.

Another related explanation is that the pig represents the demonic. As St. Athanasius records in his biography, St. Anthony experienced many attacks from the devil which sometimes came in the form of wild animals perhaps even wild pigs. And the image of wild pigs brings to mind the story in the Gospels where Jesus permitted the demons to enter the pigs who then promptly drowned themselves. (Luke 8:32-33)

A third possible association with pigs is related to skin disease. St. Anthony was known to be an intercessor for people who were who suffering from various skin diseases. The reason for that was probably because of the excellent health which he maintained throughout the course of his life in spite his ascetic lifestyle.

Skin diseases were often treated using pork fat because it would reduce the inflammation and itching. In order to make the connection between St. Anthony and his patronage for sufferers of skin diseases, the artists might have included a pig with the saint.

A later explanation is related to an order of that was founded centuries after his death—the Hospitallers of St. Anthony—who took the saint for their patron. The order was founded around 1095 by Gaston of Dauphiné who started the ministry of giving aid to the poor in thanksgiving from his own miraculous cure of a disease known as St. Anthony's Fire. The disease which is now known as ergotism was of epidemic proportions and responsible for the deaths of many in Europe over the centuries.

The order was supported in part by pigs. First, the order was allowed to raise pigs. Second, people would donate a pig to the order, raise the pig themselves, and give it to the order on the feast of St. Anthony which is the 17th of January.

Finally, there is the most appealing explanation (at least for pigs) which is that the saint healed a wild pig and through that action befriended the animal who remained with him in the desert. Of course, St. Anthony was a vegetarian so the pig would not ever have to worry about becoming his dinner.

In celebration of this story, there is a tradition of bringing domestic animals, including pigs, to the parish on January 17th in order to have them blessed by the priest.

Whichever story made the first connection between the saint and pigs, eventually pig herders latched on to his association with pigs and he became their patron as well as the patron of pigs, of course, and domestic animals, in general.

Source: "A Pig in the Desert: Why Saint Anthony the Great is Shown with a Pig." Letter From the Saints.com. 11 August 2019
https://www.lettersfromthesaints.com/blog/a-pig-in-the-desert-why-st-anthony-the-great-is-shown-with-a-pig

— 3.3 —

I'll e'en leave all, and with the patient ass,
The over-laden ass, throw off my burden,
And cast mine office; pluck in my large ears. 20
Betimes, lest some disjudge 'em to be horns.
(3.3-18-21)
Source of Above:
The Cambridge Edition of the Works of Ben Jonson
7 Volume Set. Volume 6.
Ben Jonson (Author), David Bevington (Editor), Martin Butler (Editor), Ian Donaldson (Editor).
Cambridge University Press, 2012. Print. P. 601-602.
The reference to "large ears" and "horns" comes from one of Aesop's Fables that has more than one moral:

A hurt Lion banned all horned animals from his kingdom. A Hare saw his ears looked like horns in his shadow decided to leave, ending a long-term friendship.

Paranoia can change everything.

Aesop For Children (The Hare and His Ears)

The Lion had been badly hurt by the horns of a Goat, which he was eating. He was very angry to think that any animal that he chose for a meal, should be so brazen as to wear such dangerous things as horns to scratch him while he ate. So he commanded that all animals with horns should leave his domains within twenty-four hours.

The command struck terror among the beasts. All those who were so unfortunate as to have horns, began to pack up and move out. Even the Hare, who, as you know, has no horns and so had nothing to fear, passed a very restless night, dreaming awful dreams about the fearful Lion.

And when he came out of the warren in the early morning sunshine, and there saw the shadow cast by his long and pointed ears, a terrible fright seized him.

"Goodby, neighbor Cricket," he called. "I'm off. He will certainly make out that my ears are horns, no matter what I say."

Moral

Do not give your enemies the slightest reason to attack your reputation.

Your enemies will seize any excuse to attack you.

JBR Collection

The Lion being once badly hurt by the horns of a Goat, went into a great rage, and swore that every animal with horns should be banished from his kingdom. Goats, Bulls, Rams, Deer, and every living thing with horns had quickly to be off on pain of death. A Hare, seeing from his shadow how long his ears were, was in great fear lest they should be taken for horns. "Good-bye, my friend," said he to a Cricket who, for many a long summer evening, had chirped to him where he lay dozing: "I must be off from here. My ears are too much like horns to allow me to be comfortable." "Horns!" exclaimed the Cricket, "do you take me for a fool? You no more have horns than I have." "Say what you please," replied the Hare, "were my cars only half as long as they are, they would be quite long enough for any one to lay hold of who wished to make them out to be horns."

Source of Above: Daboss, "The Hare Afraid of Its Ears." 14 May 2014
https://fablesofaesop.com/hare-afraid-ears.html
Another moral is this:

"Cowards die many times before their death."

Source: "Bedtime stories - The Hare and its Ears - stories for kids - Storytime with R." Storytime with Rajju Aunty." YouTube. 18 April 2016 https://www.youtube.com/watch?v=6uL3FbeIGKI

— 3.6 —

His name was Vadian, and a cunning Tooter.

(3.6.26)

Source of Above:

The Cambridge Edition of the Works of Ben Jonson

7 Volume Set. Volume 6.

Ben Jonson (Author), David Bevington (Editor), Martin Butler (Editor), Ian Donaldson (Editor).

Cambridge University Press, 2012. Print. P. 608.

A Fabian is a member of the Roman gens (family) Fabia. This was a patrician name.

In 321 B.C.E., Quintus Fabius Ambustus was nominated to be Dictator. A fault in the auspices forced him to resign.

In 315 B.C.E., Quintus Fabius Maximus Rullianus was Dictator.

In 216 B.C.E., Marcus Fabius Buteo was named Dictator after the Battle of Cannae in which the Carthaginian general Hannibal achieved a great victory against the Romans.

In 221 and 217 B.C.E., Quintus Fabius Maximus Verrucosis — known as Cunctator — was dictator. "Cunctator" means "Delayer," and as dictator he harassed Hannibal's army without ever fighting it in open battle. This is probably the "Vadian" To-Pan meant.

In other words:

Vadian = Fabian = Fabius

Of course, we remember:

Octavian = Octavius

— 3.9 —

At the report of it, an ox did speak,
(3.9.56)
Source of Above:
The Cambridge Edition of the Works of Ben Jonson
7 Volume Set. Volume 6.
Ben Jonson (Author), David Bevington (Editor), Martin Butler (Editor), Ian Donaldson (Editor).
Cambridge University Press, 2012. Print. P. 616.
Below is the passage from Livy that Ben Jonson used above:

> *2] Before the consul and praetors set out for their provinces, a supplication was held by reason of prodigies. [3] A she-goat was reported from Picenum to have given birth to six kids at one time, and at Arretium a boy with one hand was born, at Amiternum [4??] there was a shower of earth, at Formiae the wall and gate were struck by lightning, and, a thing which caused the greatest terror, at Rome a cow belonging to the consul Gnaeus Domitius spoke, saying, "Rome, for thyself beware."*

Source of Above:
Livy. *History of Rome.* Books XXXV-XXXVII With An English Translation. Cambridge. Cambridge, Mass., Harvard University Press; London, William Heinemann, Ltd. 1935: published without copyright notice.
https://www.perseus.tufts.edu/hopper/
text?doc=Perseus%3Atext%3A1999.02.0165%3Abook%3D35%3Achapter%3D2

— 3.9 —

The hens too cackled, at the noise whereof
  A drake was seen to dance a headless round;
  The goose was cut i'the head to hear it too.
(3.9.61-63)
Source of Above:
The Cambridge Edition of the Works of Ben Jonson
7 Volume Set. Volume 6.
Ben Jonson (Author), David Bevington (Editor), Martin Butler (Editor), Ian Donaldson (Editor).
Cambridge University Press, 2012. Print. P. 616.
Below is some information about why chickens move after their heads are cut off:

> *When you chop off a chicken's head, the pressure of the axe triggers all the nerve endings in the neck, causing that little burst of electricity to run down all the nerves leading back to the muscles, to tell them to move. The chicken appears to flap its wings and to run around — even though it's already dead.*

Source of Below:
Jan Poole, "Curious Kids: how can chickens run around after their heads have been chopped off?" *The Conversation.* 25 September 2018
https://theconversation.com/curious-kids-how-can-chickens-run-around-after-their-heads-have-been-chopped-off-103701

But if you get the lass from Dargison,
   What will you do with her?
(4.3.27-28)
Source of Above:
The Cambridge Edition of the Works of Ben Jonson
7 Volume Set. Volume 6.
Ben Jonson (Author), David Bevington (Editor), Martin Butler (Editor), Ian Donaldson (Editor).
Cambridge University Press, 2012. Print. P. 628.
According to the *Oxford English Dictionary*, this is the definition of "darg":

  A day's work, the task of a day

"Dargison" could mean "son of work," and so it could mean a working man. Here is a comment that may be relevant:

Dargasson. In Irish gasson (from the French) means de lad or boy. Though it's slightly derogatory it's far more preferable to the alternative manín that is on the point of insult.

Source of Above:
"Dargason." *The Session.* Comment by Peter.
Posted by pfiddle@gmail.com 13 years ago [2009].
https://thesession.org/tunes/9468
"The [de] lad" is the meaning of the French *le gamin* and *le garçon.*
The French *gosse* means "kid, child, brat."
Perhaps "Dargason" is "De Gascon."
"De" can mean "from" or "the."
Miles Metaphor may be a young man and so be referred to derogatorily as "the boy."
Here are two definitions of "gascon" in the *Oxford English Dictionary*:

A native or inhabitant of Gascony, a region and former province in south-west France.

A person who resembles a Gascon in character; a braggart, a boaster.

The *Oxford English Dictionary*'s first recorded instance of the second definition, however, is from 1757.

Miles Metaphor did some boasting when he said, "Had they been but some five or six, I'd whipped them all like tops in Lent, and hurled them into Hobbler's hole, or the next ditch."

But he said that to Chanon Hugh and Justice Preamble. Squire Tub would not be aware of that boasting.

APPENDIX A: FAIR USE

The use of the information in this section is consistent with fair use:

§ 107. Limitations on exclusive rights: Fair use

Release date: 2004-04-30

Notwithstanding the provisions of sections 106 and 106A, the fair use of a copyrighted work, including such use by reproduction in copies or phonorecords or by any other means specified by that section, for purposes such as criticism, comment, news reporting, teaching (including multiple copies for classroom use), scholarship, or research, is not an infringement of copyright. In determining whether the use made of a work in any particular case is a fair use the factors to be considered shall include —

(1) the purpose and character of the use, including whether such use is of a commercial nature or is for nonprofit educational purposes;

(2) the nature of the copyrighted work;

(3) the amount and substantiality of the portion used in relation to the copyrighted work as a whole; and

(4) the effect of the use upon the potential market for or value of the copyrighted work.

The fact that a work is unpublished shall not itself bar a finding of fair use if such finding is made upon consideration of all the above factors.

Source of Fair Use information:
<http://www.law.cornell.edu/uscode/17/107.html>

APPENDIX B: ABOUT THE AUTHOR

It was a dark and stormy night. Suddenly a cry rang out, and on a hot summer night in 1954, Josephine, wife of Carl Bruce, gave birth to a boy — me. Unfortunately, this young married couple allowed Reuben Saturday, Josephine's brother, to name their first-born. Reuben, aka "The Joker," decided that Bruce was a nice name, so he decided to name me Bruce Bruce. I have gone by my middle name — David — ever since.

Being named Bruce David Bruce hasn't been all bad. Bank tellers remember me very quickly, so I don't often have to show an ID. It can be fun in charades, also. When I was a counselor as a teenager at Camp Echoing Hills in Warsaw, Ohio, a fellow counselor gave the signs for "sounds like" and "two words," then she pointed to a bruise on her leg twice. Bruise Bruise? Oh yeah, Bruce Bruce is the answer!

Uncle Reuben, by the way, gave me a haircut when I was in kindergarten. He cut my hair short and shaved a small bald spot on the back of my head. My mother wouldn't let me go to school until the bald spot grew out again.

Of all my brothers and sisters (six in all), I am the only transplant to Athens, Ohio. I was born in Newark, Ohio, and have lived all around Southeastern Ohio. However, I moved to Athens to go to Ohio University and have never left.

At Ohio U, I never could make up my mind whether to major in English or Philosophy, so I got a bachelor's degree with a double major in both areas, then I added a Master of Arts degree in English and a Master of Arts degree in Philosophy. Yes, I have my MAMA degree.

Currently, and for a long time to come (I eat fruits and veggies), I am spending my retirement writing books such as *Nadia Comaneci: Perfect 10*, *The Funniest People in Comedy*, *Homer's* Iliad: *A Retelling in Prose*, and *William Shakespeare's* Hamlet: *A Retelling in Prose*.

By the way, my sister Brenda Kennedy writes romances such as *A New Beginning* and *Shattered Dreams*.

APPENDIX C: SOME BOOKS BY DAVID BRUCE

Retellings of a Classic Work of Literature

Arden of Faversham: A Retelling

Ben Jonson's The Alchemist: *A Retelling*

Ben Jonson's The Arraignment, or Poetaster: *A Retelling*

Ben Jonson's Bartholomew Fair: *A Retelling*

Ben Jonson's The Case is Altered: *A Retelling*

Ben Jonson's Catiline's Conspiracy: *A Retelling*

Ben Jonson's The Devil is an Ass: *A Retelling*

Ben Jonson's Epicene: *A Retelling*

Ben Jonson's Every Man in His Humor: *A Retelling*

Ben Jonson's Every Man Out of His Humor: *A Retelling*

Ben Jonson's The Fountain of Self-Love, or Cynthia's Revels: *A Retelling*

Ben Jonson's The Magnetic Lady, or Humors Reconciled: *A Retelling*

Ben Jonson's The New Inn, or The Light Heart: *A Retelling*

Ben Jonson's Sejanus' Fall: *A Retelling*

Ben Jonson's The Staple of News: *A Retelling*

Ben Jonson's A Tale of a Tub: *A Retelling*

Ben Jonson's Volpone, or the Fox: *A Retelling*

Christopher Marlowe's Complete Plays: Retellings

Christopher Marlowe's Dido, Queen of Carthage: *A Retelling*

Christopher Marlowe's Doctor Faustus: *Retellings of the 1604 A-Text and of the 1616 B-Text*

Christopher Marlowe's Edward II: *A Retelling*

Christopher Marlowe's The Massacre at Paris: *A Retelling*

Christopher Marlowe's The Rich Jew of Malta: *A Retelling*

Christopher Marlowe's Tamburlaine, Parts 1 and 2: *Retellings*

Dante's Divine Comedy: *A Retelling in Prose*

Dante's Inferno: *A Retelling in Prose*

Dante's Purgatory: *A Retelling in Prose*

Dante's Paradise: *A Retelling in Prose*

The Famous Victories of Henry V: *A Retelling*

From the Iliad *to the* Odyssey: *A Retelling in Prose of Quintus of Smyrna's* Posthomerica

George Chapman, Ben Jonson, and John Marston's Eastward Ho! *A Retelling*

George Peele's The Arraignment of Paris: *A Retelling*

George Peele's The Battle of Alcazar: *A Retelling*

George Peele's David and Bathsheba, and the Tragedy of Absalom: *A Retelling*

George Peele's Edward I: *A Retelling*

George Peele's The Old Wives' Tale: *A Retelling*

George-a-Greene: *A Retelling*

The History of King Leir: A Retelling

Homer's Iliad: *A Retelling in Prose*

Homer's Odyssey: *A Retelling in Prose*

J.W. Gent.'s The Valiant Scot: *A Retelling*

Jason and the Argonauts: A Retelling in Prose of Apollonius of Rhodes' Argonautica

John Ford: Eight Plays Translated into Modern English

John Ford's The Broken Heart: *A Retelling*

John Ford's The Fancies, Chaste and Noble: *A Retelling*

John Ford's The Lady's Trial: *A Retelling*

John Ford's The Lover's Melancholy: *A Retelling*

John Ford's Love's Sacrifice: *A Retelling*

John Ford's Perkin Warbeck: *A Retelling*

John Ford's The Queen: *A Retelling*

John Ford's 'Tis Pity She's a Whore: *A Retelling*

John Lyly's Campaspe: *A Retelling*

John Lyly's Endymion, The Man in the Moon: *A Retelling*

John Lyly's Galatea: *A Retelling*

John Lyly's Love's Metamorphosis: *A Retelling*

John Lyly's Midas: *A Retelling*

John Lyly's Mother Bombie: *A Retelling*

John Lyly's Sappho and Phao: *A Retelling*

John Lyly's The Woman in the Moon: *A Retelling*

John Webster's The White Devil: *A Retelling*

King Edward III: *A Retelling*

Mankind: *A Medieval Morality Play* (A Retelling)

Margaret Cavendish's The Unnatural Tragedy: *A Retelling*

The Merry Devil of Edmonton: *A Retelling*

The Summoning of Everyman: *A Medieval Morality Play* (A Retelling)

Robert Greene's Friar Bacon and Friar Bungay: *A Retelling*

The Taming of a Shrew: *A Retelling*

Tarlton's Jests: A Retelling

Thomas Middleton's A Chaste Maid in Cheapside: *A Retelling*

Thomas Middleton's Women Beware Women: *A Retelling*

Thomas Middleton and Thomas Dekker's The Roaring Girl: *A Retelling*

Thomas Middleton and William Rowley's The Changeling: *A Retelling*

The Trojan War and Its Aftermath: Four Ancient Epic Poems

Virgil's Aeneid: *A Retelling in Prose*

William Shakespeare's 5 Late Romances: Retellings in Prose

William Shakespeare's 10 Histories: Retellings in Prose

William Shakespeare's 11 Tragedies: Retellings in Prose

William Shakespeare's 12 Comedies: Retellings in Prose

William Shakespeare's 38 Plays: Retellings in Prose
William Shakespeare's 1 Henry IV, aka Henry IV, Part 1: *A Retelling in Prose*
William Shakespeare's 2 Henry IV, aka Henry IV, Part 2: *A Retelling in Prose*
William Shakespeare's 1 Henry VI, aka Henry VI, Part 1: *A Retelling in Prose*
William Shakespeare's 2 Henry VI, aka Henry VI, Part 2: *A Retelling in Prose*
William Shakespeare's 3 Henry VI, aka Henry VI, Part 3: *A Retelling in Prose*
William Shakespeare's All's Well that Ends Well: *A Retelling in Prose*
William Shakespeare's Antony and Cleopatra: *A Retelling in Prose*
William Shakespeare's As You Like It: *A Retelling in Prose*
William Shakespeare's The Comedy of Errors: *A Retelling in Prose*
William Shakespeare's Coriolanus: *A Retelling in Prose*
William Shakespeare's Cymbeline: *A Retelling in Prose*
William Shakespeare's Hamlet: *A Retelling in Prose*
William Shakespeare's Henry V: *A Retelling in Prose*
William Shakespeare's Henry VIII: *A Retelling in Prose*
William Shakespeare's Julius Caesar: *A Retelling in Prose*
William Shakespeare's King John: *A Retelling in Prose*
William Shakespeare's King Lear: *A Retelling in Prose*
William Shakespeare's Love's Labor's Lost: *A Retelling in Prose*
William Shakespeare's Macbeth: *A Retelling in Prose*
William Shakespeare's Measure for Measure: *A Retelling in Prose*
William Shakespeare's The Merchant of Venice: *A Retelling in Prose*
William Shakespeare's The Merry Wives of Windsor: *A Retelling in Prose*
William Shakespeare's A Midsummer Night's Dream: *A Retelling in Prose*
William Shakespeare's Much Ado About Nothing: *A Retelling in Prose*
William Shakespeare's Othello: *A Retelling in Prose*
William Shakespeare's Pericles, Prince of Tyre: *A Retelling in Prose*
William Shakespeare's Richard II: *A Retelling in Prose*
William Shakespeare's Richard III: *A Retelling in Prose*
William Shakespeare's Romeo and Juliet: *A Retelling in Prose*
William Shakespeare's The Taming of the Shrew: *A Retelling in Prose*
William Shakespeare's The Tempest: *A Retelling in Prose*
William Shakespeare's Timon of Athens: *A Retelling in Prose*
William Shakespeare's Titus Andronicus: *A Retelling in Prose*
William Shakespeare's Troilus and Cressida: *A Retelling in Prose*
William Shakespeare's Twelfth Night: *A Retelling in Prose*
William Shakespeare's The Two Gentlemen of Verona: *A Retelling in Prose*
William Shakespeare's The Two Noble Kinsmen: *A Retelling in Prose*
William Shakespeare's The Winter's Tale: *A Retelling in Prose*